'Beth?'

As Luca spoke her name she trembled. She knew his touch came at a price, but she no longer cared. The same wisdom that made her desperate for him also warned she would be nothing more than his next conquest. Still she could not resist.

When his fingers traced their way around the heart-shaped outline of her face, she looked up. Tears were threatening to fill her eyes, but before she could apologise for it, he kissed her.

In an instant, all her fear and pain slipped away. Desire filled the void he had left in her body. The warmth of longing infused her. It was such a long time since he had held her with genuine passion like this. She relaxed, savouring every second of the experience.

She was in Luca's arms.

Dear Reader

1908 was a wonderful year for lovers of romantic fiction. Mills and Boon was born, and over the years their books have helped millions of readers escape to a world filled with excitement, love and passion. I started reading them as a teenager, sharing the rollercoaster ride of couples overcoming all sorts of obstacles in the search for their happy-ever-after. My favourites were the stories where an independent, unconventionally attractive girl broke through the defences of her unattainable hero. They gave such hope to the stroppy, lumpen fourth-former I was in those days!

Writing for Mills and Boon was a distant dream for me then. When my first book was accepted, I could hardly believe my luck. HER RUTHLESS ITALIAN BOSS is my fourth Modern™ Romance for Harlequin Mills and Boon, and I'm still high on the excitement of it all. I hope you love the hero, Luca, as much as I do. Strong, self-reliant men have always fascinated me. As an ex-soldier, Luca is all that and more. If only he could forgive Beth for the way she treated him in the past, he would be the perfect man. But as far as Beth is concerned he's always been her ideal. If she can't have him, then she doesn't want anyone else.

I've really enjoyed making Luca into a hero to continue the Mills and Boon tradition. It's a real privilege to be writing at the beginning of the company's second century. With you, I look forward to enjoying hours of reading pleasure in the future.

With my warmest wishes

Christina

HER RUTHLESS
ITALIAN BOSS

BY
CHRISTINA HOLLIS

MILLS & BOON™®
Pure reading pleasure

First published in Great Britain 2008
Harlequin Mills & Boon Limited,
Eton House, 18-24 Paradise Road, Richmond, Surrey TW9 1SR

© Christina Hollis 2008

ISBN: 978 0 263 86447 2

Set in Times Roman 10½ on 13 pt
01-0708-48923

Printed and bound in Spain
by Litografia Rosés, S.A., Barcelona

Christina Hollis was born in Somerset, and now lives in the idyllic Wye Valley. She was born reading, and her childhood dream was to become a writer. This was realised when she became a successful journalist and lecturer in organic horticulture. Then she gave it all up to become a full-time mother of two, and to run half an acre of productive country garden. Writing Mills & Boon® romances is another ambition realised. It fills most of her time, between complicated rural school runs. The rest of her life is divided between garden and kitchen, either growing fruit and vegetables or cooking with them. Her daughter's cat always closely supervises everything she does around the home, from typing to picking strawberries!

Recent titles by the same author:

ONE NIGHT IN HIS BED
COUNT GIOVANNI'S VIRGIN
THE ITALIAN BILLIONAIRE'S VIRGIN

To Kate Walker, for all her good advice.

CHAPTER ONE

FROM the first moment she saw Venice from a waterbus, Beth was entranced. *La Serenissima* rose from the lagoon like crystals growing up through mist. If a city could be described as being like a woman, then this one was straight out of a nineteenth-century novel. Everywhere murmured with the sound of water whispering against wood and stonework. Beth could identify with all this gentle melancholy. She was miles from home, and feeling sick with fear at the prospect of arriving at the headquarters of Francesco Fine Arts for the first time. I'll love this new job once I get there, she thought, desperately trying to convince herself. She was tired, alone and scared. There had been too many challenges over the past few years. The immortal serenity of Venice was in stark contrast to the confusion of consultants and hospitals she had needed to arrange for her father. His eventual death had been so hard to bear, and the after effects had cast her adrift from all the security she knew and loved.

A wave of excitement suddenly engulfed the other passengers in her boat. Half a dozen Venetian matrons erupted with coos of admiration, and then everyone started pointing through the fine drizzle. They were all talking at once, and it didn't take long for Beth to see why. A spectacular craft was approaching. The thoroughbred's streamlined beauty swept past them with an assurance that made it seem a whole lot faster than the speed limit. The pilot drew as many admiring looks as his boat did. He was tall, lean and concentrating like a perfectionist. The fingers of one hand splayed casually against the boat's paintwork, while the other dealt with the controls. His attitude was totally out of place in that soft-focus, watercolour landscape. And yet it was strangely familiar… Beth's heart stopped dead, and amazement pitched her to her feet.

'Good grief! What's he doing here?' She gasped, before coming to her senses. People were looking at her, and grinning. Sinking back into her seat with an embarrassed grin, Beth muttered some apologies. I must be going mad with the stress of it all, she thought. Hallucinating about Luca should have stopped years ago. He was a career soldier on frontline duty, and the very *last* person who would be found piloting a luxury speedboat around Venice. As for dressing in Milan tailoring and wraparound shades—it was laughable, but that didn't dull her pain. Silenced by heartache, she watched her vision disappear into the distance, sweeping off to his own private kingdom like the royalty he obviously was.

Whoever he is, he probably didn't even see me, Beth thought.

She was right. Self-made billionaires didn't need to notice ordinary mortals. Luca Francesco was no exception. He had checked his e-mails three times already that morning, and his mind was full of schedules and appointments. Thank God Ben Simpson's pet PA was finally arriving from England today, he mused—the woman must be a saint to put up with him.

Reaching the headquarters of Francesco Fine Arts, Luca left his docking attendant to moor the craft, and strode into the building. Nodding in the direction of the reception staff, he stabbed the button of his private lift. He was still irritated by the reality of Ben Simpson. The man might be a genius in his field, but he had no common sense at all, and no social skills. Luca had merely waved through the request from FFA's Human Resources department to include Ben's girl Friday as part of his employment package. At the time, it had seemed like a harmless perk of the job. Everyone had discovered since then she must be a vital part of Ben Simpson's life-support system.

The elevator arrived. Luca stepped in, wincing as the mirrored doors clicked shut. That final glass of vin santo last night had been a mistake. He had flown to Florence, to taste Count Guido's latest vintage. As he always did, Luca had agreed with his host that the wine was even better than Guido's previous releases. He had been saying that for five years. Luca had no enthusiasm for socialising any more, but his manners were faultless—right down to accepting that last shot of alcohol. Thinking about it now made him flinch. Luckily, one of his chauffeurs had been acting as co-pilot, and had flown him back to Venice a few hours ago. There had been no time for sleep, and he had accepted Count Guido's offer of a guest wing for the night it would have pushed Luca several conversations too far.

He was a man with a thousand invitations, who had lost all desire for friendship.

And now he had to force himself to face office life—again.

Luca had been sharing his own PA, Andria, while they all waited for Ben Simpson's girl to sort out her 'personal problems' back in England. He was thinking of giving this shadowy wonder-woman an immediate pay rise, sight unseen. Feeling the way he did this morning, the next problem Luca met with Ben was liable to end with blood being spilled all over the executive carpet…

By the time she reached her new workplace, Beth's heart was hammering so fast, she thought it might burst. Ben had arranged to meet her in the vestibule and escort her up to their office suite. He led her through a busy honeycomb of activity. Although it was set within a rambling old building, full of cubby-holes and squeaking floorboards, everything at FFA ran with the high-tech efficiency of an international multibillion-dollar business. While firewalls and virus checkers protected investments, the building's real walls were draped with tapestries. As she was shown around Beth wondered if the drapes hid any secret passages. The people who lived here in the Renaissance had been high on security—in those days, lives as well as fortunes were at stake. Ben guided her through a warren of passages, stopping every so often to ask directions back to his office. Beth didn't mind. It gave her a chance to admire her surroundings. Beautiful antique side tables and grand carved chairs were placed at regular intervals along each corridor. Her father would have loved it. He had adored treasures, and this place was stuffed with them. Each time he had gone out to buy stock, Gerald Woodbury had brought home at least one more exquisite piece he could not bear to put up for sale. Unfortunately, his bank account had emptied at much the same speed with which his beloved Rose Cottage had filled up with beautiful things.

As soon as they reached their office Beth plunged straight into her job of making Ben's life run as smoothly as possible. Their suite had been formed out of the building's old ballroom, and it did not take her long to convince him that his desk should be repositioned, right at the far end. He was too easily distracted to have his seat any closer to the door. Her workstation would stand guard there, fending off unwanted visitors.

Disaster struck only a short time after they had settled down to work. A frantic call drifted over to where Beth was setting up some computer records.

'Beth—Beth—I've just sat on my glasses!'

'The spare pair is in the top right-hand drawer of your desk, as always.'

'This *is* the spare pair! I lost a lens from the other ones just after I got here…'

Beth picked up the telephone on her desk and made a quick call. Then she walked over and handed Ben a note.

'Don't panic. Here are the details of your new English-speaking optician. They're expecting you.'

Ben beamed, stood up and pulled on his jacket. 'If ever Signor Francesco wants to know why I need you here, I'll tell him about little things like this!'

Seconds after Ben left, Beth came to his rescue again when the telephone on his desk rang.

'Oh—hi, you must be Beth!' a friendly voice said. 'I'm Andria, Signor Francesco's assistant. Could you send Ben up to the executive lounge, please? Signor Francesco wants to see the notes for his address to the ceramics convention next month. I thought the two of them could cosy up over a latte.'

'Oh, I'm sorry, Andria, Ben's had to dash out for a while—'

Beth heard a sharp intake of breath from her opposite number. That was a clear danger signal, and nothing could be allowed to blot Ben's reputation. Beth sprang into action.

'But I can deliver the notes myself. I've got them right here, and they're all ready.'

'Brilliant.' Andria's relief was audible. 'Signor Francesco is a good boss, but he's totally single-minded when it comes to work. If he thought I'd sent him on a coffee break without the chance of fitting in a bit of paper-work, I'd never hear the end of it!'

Beth laughed, printed out the document and slipped it into a cover. It sounded as though she would have her work cut out keeping Ben on the right side of his boss. No wonder he had wanted her help and support in this new job. Ben was as disorganised as he was accident-prone. She had better get out of her silly habit of wincing each time she heard the surname of their new employer.

When Ben had announced the people at Francesco Fine Arts had approached him, Beth's stomach had gone into a spin. The simple mention of a name shared by millions of people around the globe had thrown her into turmoil. Then reality had supplied a parachute, and told her not to be so stupid. Luca had been a soldier, and the original bull in a china shop. What connection could he possibly have with international fine art? The only interest he ever showed in glass was how much liquid it could hold. All the same, Beth was still not comfortable hearing the name 'Francesco'. It would be a relief to meet their new managing director at last. When his real-life image replaced the tall, dark fury that still haunted her, life would become easier.

Negotiating the maze of corridors, Beth was scared in case her rusty holiday Italian let her down, but everyone she met in the building was really friendly. She soon found the executive lounge, and walked in with a broad smile.

It evaporated the instant she saw the man who was silhouetted at the window. The impressive figure had his back to her, but she still recognised him. He was the same man who had been piloting that speedboat, and the realisation hit her heart a hammer blow. Now there could be no mistake. His sable-dark hair had not been given its regulation trim in a while and now curled almost to his collar, but it didn't matter. Beth was convinced that when the managing director of Francesco Fine Arts turned around, every word, English or Italian, would desert her. She already knew this billionaire workaholic would turn out to be the man she desired most in the world.

And the only one she would ever love.

Beth had been quiet and discreet, but Luca still heard her enter the room. He glanced over his shoulder with a smile—and then stopped. In one second his open expression turned from pleasure to deep, dark distrust. Beth went cold with dread. Although he was not handsome in the way of soap stars or male models, Luca was devastating to look at. Those dark, wide-set eyes might have lashes to die for, but the effect was compelling, not sentimental. His masculinity was carved, not manufactured. It had been honed on the assault course, giving him a form every woman wanted to touch. Beth was no exception. Despite his ten-kilowatt glare, the first thing she noticed was how pale and tired he looked.

And then his quiet words tore the years away.

'*Mio Dio*...I must have died and gone to hell...'

Beth was shattered. His eyes were like chips of black diamond. The man who meant everything to her was now trying to intimidate her, not melt her. He succeeded in no time at all, because Beth's soul still bore the indelible brand of his hard, dark anger. It had been seared into her on that last burning night in Balacha. Five years later, it still hurt.

She began inching pinches along the edge of the file she carried, measuring her embarrassment and shame.

'Luca...I had no idea...I would never have come here if I'd known—'

He silenced her with a single, sharp gesture of his hand. Their time apart had increased his natural authority a hundredfold. His appearance had always been unconventional. Now he looked dangerous. Instead of tanned and open, his face was drawn and watchful. Those beautiful eyes with their sweeping lashes now had dark hollows beneath them. Beth was horrified, but all the old attraction was still there. She could sense it, but she could also feel waves of resentment flowing from him.

Shock and shame forced her words out in a torrent of

apology. 'Look, I can hardly blame you for being angry with me, Luca. I picked up a pen a thousand times to try and write to you but—'

'Don't give me any more lies, Elizabeth. Or Beth, or whatever your name is these days. I don't need your excuses.' His tone was like silk drawn over sandpaper. 'I suppose you must be this indispensable PA Ben Simpson needs to keep him in check?' He moved forward. Beth stepped back. Seeing her flinch, he exhaled angrily. 'There's no point in pretending to be afraid of me. We both know that's never been the case. Besides, what's done is done. As far as I am concerned you are part of my past, and a part that I have no wish to remember. My interest is in the here and now.'

He paused, and raised his right hand to the side of his head. Beth watched him dig his fingers into his temple before continuing. 'I won't go back on the agreement to employ you. Ben is fast becoming a world expert in ceramics. I want him on my team and, for that privilege, I am willing to endure anything. Even your presence,' he finished meaningfully.

Somehow, Beth pulled herself together. Over the past couple of years she had survived a lot, but much of it had not been of her own making. Luca's cold fury was a different thing altogether. This was entirely down to her, so she would just have to put a brave face on it.

'Don't worry—now I can see how things are, I won't be staying here for more than six months. That's the length of my initial contract with FFA, and I won't be asking you to renew it. I wouldn't dream of putting you to any trouble, Signor Francesco.' She managed to keep her voice calm, but her mind was in chaos. All she knew was that she had to escape from his presence, to get away…

'But while you are here, you will give every assistance to Ben in his job as my new Head of Glassware and Ceramics.'

It was a command, not a question.

'Of course. That's why you are employing me, Signor Francesco,' Beth replied crisply. 'But I shall make arrangements to train a replacement, so I can leave the moment my contract comes up for renewal.'

'As long as we both know where we stand,' Luca said grimly. He paused as if he wanted to say more, but then turned away from her. 'Let me call for some refreshments.'

One end of the executive lounge had been fitted out as a kitchen, making everything from antipasti to zabaglione. Beth tucked the file of paperwork under her arm and set off to fetch him something. Any good PA would have done the same, but she intended this as a statement as well. She wanted to show Luca she knew her place as a loyal employee.

'I'll fetch you a latte and—'

'Elizabeth, you don't have to wait on me. Please find yourself a seat.'

Beth had never thought of Luca's Italian accent as dynamite before. Now it was enough to send her hurtling towards one of the softly upholstered settees scattered around the room. She sat down, her eyes fixed on the edge of the table in front of her. It was piled with magazines, but she was not in the mood to look at them. After summoning a waitress and giving his instructions, Luca rejoined her. He did not sit on the settee. Instead he picked up a hard, angular chair and dropped it opposite where she was retreating into the shelter of comfortable cushions. Although he tried to hide it, Beth saw him wince. She wondered if he was in pain but thought better than to ask. The waitress, in a smart lavender apron, brought a tray to their table. The girl set down two cups of coffee and two pastries, laying a mono-grammed napkin and fork beside each place.

When he saw she had brought nothing else, Luca clicked his tongue and began to lever himself up from his chair.

'I'll fetch you a spoon, Elizabeth,' he murmured.

'No! No, I can manage with just a fork,' she said frantically, looking from Luca to the waitress and back again.

'Nonsense.' Luca switched on his old, devastating smile as he turned to the girl who had brought their order. 'Miss Woodbury always eats with a spoon as well as a fork, Bella. It is her good English breeding.'

Beth burned with shame. She could not remember the last time she had been able to afford to eat pudding, let alone worry about how to do it.

'Times change, Luca,' she muttered when he returned from a trip to the counter for more cutlery.

'I know. That is why you went off with the man who called himself my friend.'

'It was a big mistake.'

'As I told you at the time.'

Beth paused as she went to pick up her spoon and said softly, 'I would never have thought you were mean-minded enough to say "I told you so", Luca.'

Pained, she turned her head away. She could not afford to let him see how much he still affected her.

He paused, grazing his lower lip with his teeth. 'You're right, of course. I should not have gone so far. But you must admit, it was not without provocation, Elizabeth.'

'Please call me Beth. I prefer it nowadays,' she said faintly. 'I've given up on formality.'

'I find that hard to believe.'

Luca picked up his pastry fork and cut through the mouth-watering dessert, but Beth noticed something.

'Wait, Luca, they've only given you a small portion. Here—take mine—it's much bigger.'

'This is the way I like it.' He spoke without looking at her. 'I don't eat so much these days.'

I can see that, Beth thought, eyeing him with concern. His suit was expensively tailored, but this new-style Luca was built like a greyhound rather than the mastiff she had known back in Balacha.

'There isn't much call for route marches and midnight manoeuvres in Venice,' he added by way of explanation.

'I'll bet your girlfriend is pleased.'

He shrugged. 'They don't complain.'

His casual reply gave Beth almost as much of a shock as the way he looked at her before speaking again.

'You used to do a lot of that, didn't you, Elizabeth? Complaining, I mean.'

'Can you blame me?' she countered before looking pointedly at the fine lines of his linen jacket. 'And you don't want to lose too much more weight, Luca.'

Without breaking eye contact, he put one hand over Beth's, and removed her plate. A wave of excitement broke over her as she felt the rough, parched touch of his finger-tips, once so familiar but now moving with clinical precision.

'It doesn't take much to convince me.' He nodded, replacing her portion with his own, smaller one.

'Then it's a good job I'm not hungry.'

He sat back and laughed. 'Oh! That was almost a retort. And I thought something must have extinguished your spark, Beth. Perhaps I was wrong, for once.'

'No.' Beth scowled, remembering just how infuriating one of his greatest talents had always been. 'You were right, as always. It's just that life has doused me pretty well over the past few years.'

Beth could hardly hold Luca's piercing gaze as he answered, 'Then welcome to the club.' He sat back, his legs stretched out in front of him. 'When the army let me go, I had no alternative other than to come here to Venice. This was my great-uncle's firm. He died a couple of years ago, and left everything to me. His home—and his business, which I have developed into the success you see now.'

Beth gaped, still trying to catch up.

'Luca—you *left* the army?'

'I didn't say that.'

She stared at him. All sorts of images tumbled through her head. They must have thrown him out for some reason. She knew he had a short fuse. But he had always managed to control his temper, when they were together.

When they were together…

What on earth had she started, the night she had abandoned him in Balacha?

'But…the army was your family.'

'They had to let me go.' His features were unreadable as he took a small container from the breast pocket of his jacket and shook out a couple of small white tablets.

'Oh, Luca…'

He took no notice, but concentrated on taking the pain-killers. Beth moved forward, but he stopped her by stabbing a finger on the table between them. It was a noisy gesture of ownership.

'Don't worry about me. I have all this now.'

His hand had landed on the cover of the latest *Time* magazine, and she wondered if he was grinding in a further insult. A haunting photograph of Luca's face gazed up at her, above the headline EUROPE'S RICHEST MAN. Now he had money, and she had none. There's irony for you, Beth thought bitterly.

'I can only hope you have better luck than I've had, Luca.'

'Luck has nothing to do with it.' His eyes burned into her like glowing coals. 'Nobody has ever been lower than I was when they brought me back here, five years ago. From a position of authority, travelling the world, and fending for myself, I was reduced to nothing more than a poor relation. Worse than that, I was trapped indoors for twenty-four hours a day.' Despite his story, there was no self-pity in him. His low laugh was a dry, humourless sound. 'That didn't last long, believe me. I whipped myself, and Francesco Fine Arts, into shape at the same time. Nothing stops me, Elizabeth. Not even life. And certainly not you,' he finished meaningfully.

She looked away from him and the intensity of his words, focusing instead on the delicate pastry in front of her. Principles were slippery things when it came to luxury, and she had not tasted cake like this for a very long time. At last she came to the crumbs, then put down her spoon and fork. There was nothing for it now but to try and make a dignified exit from Luca's watchful presence.

'Well, delightful though this has been, Signor Francesco, I've delivered Ben's notes so I really must be getting back to my work,' she said in a cool, detached voice. 'Is there anything else you would like to discuss with me?'

'No.'

'I mean with regard to Ben's conference notes.'

'So do I.' He checked his Rolex. It was identical in design to the one she had presented to him, all those years ago.

Given the look in his eyes, it was probably not *exactly* the same watch.

His glance flicked across the table. He was clearly waiting for her to add something. But Beth's heart was hammering so hard in her chest that speech was impossible. For an instant she wondered if he could hear it, too. As she looked into those deep, dark, irresistible eyes it brought back the delicious thrill of his hand moving over hers a few moments before. All of a sudden, nothing mattered to her any more except winning his forgiveness, so she could have that sensation again. Then reality hit home. Luca was the boss in more ways than one now. She was nothing more than the hired hand. She would have to stifle her own feelings—all of them.

'I'd better get back to work, Signor Francesco. I always match my hours to Ben.' She met his stare calmly. 'He won't take a midday break today because he's had to go out for an optician's appointment, so I won't, either.'

Luca did not look impressed. 'You must eat, Beth. I

shall tell the staff to expect you here at one o'clock. That is the time you eat at Rose Cottage, yes?'

His expression was severe, but then she remembered how she had always managed to get around him in the past. And his mention of Rose Cottage seemed like a reminder of their time together. As she handed him the copy of Ben's notes she risked everything.

'That almost sounded like an invitation to lunch, Luca.'

'No.' He shook his head and turned away from her. 'Not today, Beth. Perhaps some other time, eh? *Ciao, bella!*'

Hope flickered again, until Beth realised his last remark was not directed at her. He was raising a hand in salute to the waitress who had served them. Beth watched him go, but he didn't once look back at her. Luca was abandoning her in the same brisk way he left the room. He could not wait to get back to a world in which she had no place at all. It was the ultimate dismissal.

CHAPTER TWO

BETH continued to stare after Luca until the door of the executive lounge eased itself closed. That broke her trance, but she gave him a few minutes to get back to his eyrie before leaving the room herself. To meet him a second time so soon after that brush-off would be awful. She needed time to steady her nerves before she saw him again. Burying herself in the reassurance of work would help. As she walked back to her desk she wondered how long it would be before she could face Luca with courage. A long time, a small, sad voice replied.

From that moment on, Beth could not concentrate properly. She had always wondered if Luca still hated her. Now she knew. He had made it clear exactly how deep his feelings ran. He had every right to feel that way. Painful though it was, she would have to isolate herself from him as much as possible. She did not want to increase his bitterness. The only way to cope was to forget they had ever meant anything to each other. She would have to stifle all her emotions, and treat him with nothing but cold formality.

But something was busily working away at the back of

her mind. It would not leave her alone, and fizzled through her body like a slow charge. The sensation grew as the day wore on until her limbs were as heavy as her head. An uncomfortable truth was beginning to seep along her veins. It mingled with the hot, urgent feeling that had leapt into life the moment she recognised him. The combination was sensual, yet terrifying. She had never stopped loving Luca, so it was no wonder her body melted now at the thought of him. What shocked Beth to the core of her being was the discovery that, no matter how much he hated her, no matter how much his attitude towards her had altered, or the weight of her own guilt—nothing changed the way she reacted to him. She still wanted him as much as ever.

Instead of going up to the executive lounge at lunchtime, Beth slipped out of the building. The thought of bumping into Luca and being trapped by his turbulent gaze again made her feel sick. It was partly embarrassment, but mostly shame. She was angry her body was not strong enough to resist him. Five years ago he had refused to make any commitment to her. Now he was blaming *her,* because she had stood up for her principles, and given him an ultimatum. And the worst part of it was, Beth knew those principles would crumble into dust now, the instant he laid another finger on her…

In the end she had to give herself a mental pep talk. I'm worth more than this, she thought, grinding her teeth so hard her head began to throb. Mooning after a man who hates me is a fast track to heartache.

She threw all her energy into her work, but it was no use. No matter how many jobs she found to do around the office that afternoon, the memory of Luca haunted her for the rest of the day. Each time there was a knock at the door her head jerked up in alarm. Every ringing telephone set her nerves jangling. She was so glad to see Ben pull his jacket off the back of his chair and try out his *'Ciao!'* at the end of the day she almost pushed him out of the door.

Beth had been so desperate to plunge into the ordeal of her first day at work she had travelled straight from the airport to the office. There had been no time to find her new home. Once she had cleared her desk and pulled the cover over her computer monitor, it was time for her second shift to begin. This time, Beth's job title was 'Apartment Hunter'.

Trying to track down the flat Ben had rented for her was a nightmare. By the time she had puzzled out his hopeless directions, it was raining and she was soaked. The 'apartment' turned out to be little more than twenty square metres of furnished hell, on the sad side of town. The agency employed by Ben had thrown Beth's few pieces of luggage into the middle of the dirty carpet. The whole room had a dank, unfriendly feel, and smelled of mushrooms. It looked as cheerful as Beth felt.

At least I won't have time to feel sorry for myself, she thought, dropping her handbag and going over to the single small window. It was sticky with disuse and she had to force it open. No refreshing breeze burst in from outside: only the relentless rattle of raindrops on rusting ironwork. She gazed down onto a cobbled courtyard, wondering how long it would be before all the puddles joined up to make a lake. A single pigeon hunched on next-door's window ledge, fluffed up against the deluge. It looked sick. Desperate for company, Beth wondered if she ought to try

and coax it closer. Before she could try, a knock at her door
sent the bird rocketing off into the rain.

The thought of having a conversation with a real person
made Beth throw common sense after the bird. Crossing
her room in a couple of strides, she opened the door and
instantly the smile froze on her face.

It was Luca.

The impulse to throw her arms around his neck and beg
to be rescued died as she saw the look in his eyes. It nailed
her to the spot. He looked as though he would respond only
too quickly, but not in the way she needed. Beth wanted to
keep him there, not send him away. She stared at him for
what felt like hours. He had changed out of his business
suit, but Luca in casual clothes looked equally stunning.
Dressed in beautifully cut jeans and a blue open necked
shirt, he was glittering with raindrops. They sparkled in his
jet-black hair and darkened his trousers to navy, but could
not dilute his disapproval. There was a bottle of Bardolino
in his left hand and a pizza box in his right, but he lowered
them as Beth's hand went to her hair. Subconsciously, her
fingers searched for the honey-blonde strands she always
twiddled when she was nervous.

'H-how in the world did you know where to find me?'
She gasped.

'Employee records.' Concern creased his brow. 'Don't
you know how dangerous it is to open your door without
finding out who is calling first, Beth? I might have been
anybody.'

For a second Beth allowed herself to think that his
concern might mean he still cared, but quickly realised that
he was just protecting his investment—doing his job.

'I heard you skipped lunch. It's a bad habit, Beth. Accept this as a peace-offering. We shouldn't have parted on such bad terms this morning, after so long apart.' His words were meant kindly enough, but his expression didn't soften.

Beth nodded, and backed into her room. This was the ultimate reversal of fortune, and it hurt.

'I—I'm sorry about the state of this place, Luca…'

'Don't be. I've seen worse.'

Both of them silently added the words 'in Balacha', but that was not something to be spoken out loud.

'Ben insisted on booking my accommodation himself, and the agency made some sort of mix-up. Apparently,' she said, staring at her sandals.

'They found him a cosy canal-side hotel room, I notice.'

Beth made a nervous, fluttering gesture with her hands. 'It doesn't matter. Sit down, Luca.'

The choice was between her apartment's squashy old armchair, and the edge of her bed. Beth pointed to the chair. Luca remained standing.

'Your reactions puzzle me, Beth.' He hesitated over her name, still finding it unusual. 'It's almost as though you really have changed since we were together.'

'I told you so.'

He raised a dark brow. 'So you are throwing my own taunt back at me, eh?'

She took the pizza from him and set it down on the apartment's single table. Opening the cutlery drawer, she tried to take out a knife, but recoiled in horror. Without comment, Luca moved in to do it for her. A previous tenant had left everything in the drawer horribly sticky. Luca went over to the small, scratched sink but could find no washing-up liquid. Cleaning the knife as best he could, he rinsed it well under a noisy, intermittent stream of tepid water. Returning it to Beth, he watched her divide up the pizza with the care she always used when she knew he was watching.

He accepted a single slice and as he watched her nibble nervously on her piece commented, 'Perhaps I shouldn't have bothered bringing a full-sized one. Knowing you, Beth, you'll throw the rest away as soon as I've disappeared.'

'I would never do a thing like that now.' She blushed, remembering all the times she had been flippant about money, dining out and always after something new.

'Really?' He raised his eyebrows in a knowing gesture.

'Really,' she repeated with feeling.

'I hope this "new" Beth is still as keen on parties as she always used to be,' he said. 'I've decided to throw one to introduce Ben to all the people who matter. As his assistant, you're invited as well, of course. It will be a chance for you to do some socialising, fine dining, and dancing— all the things that mean so much to you.'

So that's the only reason he's come to see me, Beth thought, absolutely deflated. When she had first opened the door to find Luca standing there, it had taken all her strength not to weep with relief. Thank goodness she hadn't. She made the necessary effort and forced herself to smile.

'So…when is it, exactly?'

'I haven't decided yet. I came to consult you first. How much notice does it take to get Ben to the right place at the right time?'

She looked at him scornfully, but he was quick to cut short any smart remark she might have made.

'It had better be on Friday night, or Saturday. That's for the benefit of the guests coming from abroad.'

'How much notice will they need?'

He gazed at her, quizzically. 'What do you mean?'

'People will need to check their diaries, and make arrangements.'

He raised his eyebrows, shaking his head in mystification. 'It's never bothered them before. Andria rings around. If they're free, they come. If they're not, they don't. Though I can't remember ever having a refusal.'

No, thought Beth. I'm sure you can't.

'As you obviously don't have any strong objections, I'll go ahead. This weekend is good for me. I'll ring Andria now, and she'll get things going.'

'You're off duty, but your assistant is still at work?' Beth gasped.

Luca was offended. 'Of course not—what do you think I am?'

I know exactly what you are—whatever you're doing, you're bound to be a workaholic, Beth thought. She watched him extract a phone from the pocket of his jeans. They were cut to perfection. Memories of his beautiful body had been haunting her since their first meeting in the executive lounge. Now they struck her low down, with a vengeance. Her temperature began to rise as she saw the fabric stretched tight around the tempting curve of his flank. Luckily, Luca was too busy with his call to notice the effect it was having on her.

He looked over in Beth's direction and smiled, but she

had more sense than to think it was directed at her. It must have been the stream of words chattering from his handset that sparked his amusement. Beth could imagine what poor Andria felt like, being telephoned at home on office business.

She turned away to make sure their call was private but, in a room as small as hers, it was impossible.

'Ah, yes, you know me too well,' she heard Luca say. 'That's why you're my assistant, Andria.' As he spoke he cast his eyes around Beth's new flat. 'Andria, I don't see any signs that the firm has sent Beth a welcome basket—you know the sort of thing—flowers, a few basics like coffee and washing-up liquid, fruit, a guide to local attractions…'

Luca finished his call. Beth turned to watch him put his phone back into his pocket again, although she was careful to keep her expression bland.

'Andria is the best assistant I have ever had. That girl is a mind-reader.' His satisfaction was obvious.

'That isn't quite as tricky as you might think, Luca. All it would take is for her to sacrifice everything for the sake of your career.'

His smile evaporated. 'Ah, so you still think you made the right decision in leaving me? Then you haven't seen everything my hard work has brought me. Come on—I'll show you now.' Dragging out his phone again, he called up his pilot and arranged to be picked up. 'He'll be docking my launch in ten minutes,' he informed Beth. 'If you want to grab that bottle and the pizza, we can eat later.'

Beth had to hurry to keep up with Luca as they left her apartment. His long strides led her beneath festoons of washing threaded over the back lanes. It had all been abandoned to the rain. That had stopped, but the laundry still dripped reminders of the deluge onto their heads. These alleys were hidden away, where the tourists did not visit. It was the dim, claustrophobic Venice only local people saw. Beth was glad when they reached the canal. She was even happier to recognise the smart new craft Luca had been driving earlier that day. He helped her in, his grasp firm and warm as his hand closed over hers. Beth tensed at his touch, but he let her go the moment she was safely on board. As their pilot steered them away from the mooring an argument broke out between a tenant of one of the waterside apartments and a boatman below. It resulted in a bucket of water being thrown out of an upstairs window, complete with vegetable peelings.

Beth was not impressed, and wrinkled her nose. 'I thought Venice was supposed to be more sophisticated than this.'

'Winter is coming. Tempers get shorter as the nights get longer. But it is not always like this. You will soon grow to love the place, all year round.'

'My contract with Francesco Fine Arts comes up for renewal in six months' time.'

He made no further comment and, hurt, Beth stayed silent until their launch swung around a gentle bend. Then she gasped, and Luca's smile showed his satisfaction.

'So you like my new house?'

'That's *yours?*' Beth could hardly speak. Ahead of them, a beautiful creamy-pink palace rose out of the water. Despite the cloudy sky, its four storeys were still a shimmering reflection of grace and ageless beauty.

'Oh, Luca…it's wonderful…' she breathed.

His smile had an ironic twist. 'She's falling to bits. And sinking. It would be cheaper to have the whole place transported over to the mainland, stone by stone. There, we could at least use modern luxuries like solid foundations.' He clicked his tongue. 'I don't know. This place eats money. I have to spend my working days stuck inside an office—the things I do to keep my family name alive.'

Beth thought back to the one and only time Luca had taken her backpacking. He was born to be wild. It took imagination to see him enjoying life in a perfectly proportioned, stone and shuttered place like this, lovely though it was.

'You kept very quiet about this grand family of yours when I knew you first, Luca.'

'My background wasn't important to me then. At that point there was no more than this old wreck to inherit. Besides, you were quite happy playing the part of a grand lady consorting with her "bit of rough", back then.'

The pilot tied up their launch. As Luca stepped off the boat he extended his hand to help Beth ashore. She hesitated, nervous of the effect of his touch, but she had no choice. As she suspected, when her fingers met his her body betrayed her and wanted more of what she couldn't have.

When they were both safely on the broad paved way in front of the palazzo, Luca dismissed his pilot with a smile. Now they were alone together. Beth could not stand the silence.

'I really am sorry for what happened between us in Balacha, Luca,' she said quietly.

'I don't doubt it.'

He was studying the façade of his house in minute detail.

'Can't you look at me, Luca?'

Dropping his gaze to her face, he looked at her with all the emotion of a professional poker player. 'How's that?'

'I did a stupid thing back then. It was in the heat of the moment, because I was angry. Tristram was always there. You weren't. Then one day it all got too much for me.'

Eyes burning, she looked to him for sympathy, or at least understanding. She saw neither. Luca was listening to her, but his expression showed he simply no longer cared. My God, she thought, his hidden, gentle heart has turned to stone. I might as well be explaining the running order at an English gymkhana.

'So…the way I treated you hasn't affected you at all, Luca?'

'It was a long time ago, Beth. I am over it now.'

'Is that all you can say?'

He heaved an exasperated sigh. 'Opposites attract, Beth. You moved on when you discovered we did not differ quite as much as you thought. We both like to get our own way. It's called inflexibility, and that is not a good ingredient in relationships. Or so I am told.'

'And you honestly believe that?'

'Yes,' he said slowly, 'I believe that.'

She stared at him, staggered by his uncaring attitude. She did what she always did, and fell back on good manners.

'I think—I think that as you have been kind enough to bring me here, Luca, I would like to see inside your home.'

CHAPTER THREE

LUCA led her towards his house without a word. This was another change in him. In the past, he used to laugh at her interest in bricks and mortar. Beth expected him to make some remark about her obsession with places and things, but he said nothing. As he wasn't in the army any more, she supposed he could not argue about settling in one place. But this giant step into prestige property ownership must have stretched even Luca's powers. Beth marvelled to see the great doors of the palazzo sweep apart before them, as though he had said 'open sesame'. Efficient staff met them on the threshold. Two of them took charge of the pizza and wine Beth and Luca had brought back, while another whisked Beth's jacket away. The palazzo was far too grand to have anything as simple as a coat-stand. Instead, her jacket was slipped onto a padded hanger and placed carefully inside an enormous mahogany closet.

Whatever Beth felt about Luca's silence faded the moment she stepped inside his house. Her first sight of his home knocked all the breath from her body. It really was a palace. Large winged lions topped each lintel, looking down on everyone with aristocratic scorn. Any surface that was not polished to a glass-like finish glittered with gold leaf. The entrance hall was high and wide, but Beth could hardly take it all in. She was too busy admiring the floor. It was a cold sea of marble, which gave the whole space an echoing, church-like feel. The grey-veined ground was inlaid with coloured geometric shapes of sienna and cypress, all worked into a beautiful repeating design.

'The stone was brought here from many different quarries,' Luca said, noticing her interest as he guided her past statues of his ancestors. 'When I was at school in England, the boys would bring back souvenirs from their exotic foreign vacations. I was not lucky enough to have that sort of family. My guardians arranged for me to stay in the boarding house, even during holidays. To go anywhere more romantic than Windsor was unthinkable for me then. But now…'

Hesitation was not usually part of his nature. Beth glanced at him. She had never seen wonder in his face before, but his expression came close to it now as he looked around his great vaulted hall, lavish with the art of Renaissance masters. Then he realised she was looking at him. In a flash he was back to his normal, decisive self.

'This must be the ancient version of holiday keepsakes. A reminder of all the trading missions my ancestors made to far-flung places like Asia, Egypt and Greece. I am lucky to have the job of protecting it all for future generations.'

'It sounds as though you really love this palazzo.' Beth smiled at the pride in his voice. Luca shrugged his shoulders, but the action seemed more like someone who was adjusting to a heavy burden.

'I am growing to like it. This building and all the people

who have lived here in the past must not be forgotten. Tradition is important. To me it is vital, as I grew up without any sense of close family. This place is a treasure, so, even if I would rather spend my time out in the fresh air, I owe it to my ancestors to put the needs of their palazzo first.'

'And the generations that will follow you?' Beth suggested, but he did not seem to hear. Instead he sauntered on, through to an inner courtyard. Here, herringbone brickwork and cool colonnades surrounded a high stone font, richly carved with shields and heraldic lions. Everywhere showed the chips and scratches of centuries, giving it the beauty of experience.

'When this house was built, the architects thought of everything. I even have my own well.' Luca indicated the central stone structure.

Beth stepped up onto its plinth and planted her hands on the gritty surface of the well's wide stone lip. Leaning forward, she looked over the edge.

'I can't see the bottom. How deep is it?'

Luca shrugged. 'It was intended as a private water supply in times of siege, so it has to be deep enough to make it secure.'

Inspired, Beth glanced at him again. This time she risked a smile.

'Does it grant wishes?'

Luca narrowed his eyes and gave her a look that was enough to melt any woman, and Beth was lost. Her heart hesitated, and then almost stopped as he raised one dark eyebrow.

'Try it, and see,' he murmured.

She didn't need to be told twice. Rapidly churning through the contents of her bag, she managed to find a single Euro and tossed it into the blackness. Luca watched with amusement as she craned over the edge, listening, and then smiled at her childlike excitement at the resulting 'plop'.

She caught him watching her, and sparkled.

'I really hope it works, Luca.'

A warm glow began to stroke over her body. It shimmered with tension, and she blushed. If he can read my mind I'm in trouble now, she thought breathlessly. Although not the sort of trouble I would want to avoid...

'Oh, it does, Beth. In fact, that well works a lot harder than many people I know,' he said, already starting off up a narrow stone stairway leading to the next floor. 'No visitor can resist testing its powers by throwing in money, so we dredge it regularly. The coins we pull out help to pay the bills.'

'Luca!' Beth laughed, running to catch him up. 'And you used to be so romantic!'

His laughter echoed off the ancient walls. 'Experience has taken its toll on me, *cara*.'

Beth's heart bounced again at the casual endearment. Then she caught sight of his expression. It was full of pride in ownership, nothing more. She should have known better. Luca never put his real feelings into words until it was far, far too late. Of all people, *I* should know that, she thought. Lost in memories, she hardly took in anything as Luca escorted her around a series of ever more stately apartments. She was so distracted when he merely waved a hand in the direction of his own rooms, she did not ask to

see them. It was only when they reached a separate wing
of the building she managed to rouse herself.

'This is where the official tour ends,' he said with some
relief. 'These final rooms have always been called
Tiepolo's bridal suite, as he is supposed to have been the
last decorator.'

Beth guessed Luca was trying to make a point by
running down the work of such a grand artist, so she said
nothing. Stepping past him, she went straight into the suite.
It was dark in the reception area. The still air was heavy
with the fragrance of lavender. She stopped, afraid of
blundering into anything in the gloom. Luca strode straight
past her and, one by one, opened all the pairs of tall shutters
at the far side of the room. Watery evening sunshine
streamed in and, despite all the other wonders she had
seen, Beth gasped. She was stunned.

For a few seconds, all she could do was walk around in
a small circle, gazing at the high, graceful beauty of the
apartment.

'I thought the rest of your home was lovely, but this
place is truly magical,' she breathed, lost in wonder. The
entire ceiling was decorated with exquisitely painted
gods and goddesses billowing across pink and silver
clouds. Every surface was transformed into heaven.
Wandering on into the suite, Beth was glad the click of
her stilettos was silenced here. It would have been an in-
trusion. Thick antique rugs softened the cold acreage of
marble, and muffled the echoes that made the rest of the
palazzo feel so formal and unwelcoming. All the carpet-
ing here was in shades of rose and old gold. The softly
upholstered chairs picked up these colours and every-

thing was reflected in the highly polished sheen of ancient oak furniture.

Beth walked from the reception area into the private apartments in a daze. At the heart of the suite stood an enormous bridal bed, canopied with gauze and lace hangings. These fell in sumptuous folds from somewhere near the ceiling, and she looked up to see how it was done. Then she began to have second thoughts about her dream apartment.

'It's awfully dark up there. Are you sure there aren't any bats?'

'Anyone would think you were afraid, Beth.'

'No,' she retorted nervously. 'It's just that…'

He laughed. 'Let me put your mind at rest. Though…I think electric light is too harsh for such a setting, don't you?'

Beth heard a rasping sound and light flared in the dusky gloom. It danced over a golden crown, suspended high among the ancient, smoke-blackened beams of the ceiling. She turned to see what Luca was doing. He had lit a candle. Setting it into a sconce on the wall, he took several more candles from a drawer and touched their wicks alight from the first flame. Shadows leapt up all around, moving softly through the evening light.

'Your apartments are on the other side of the building where it's so formal and cold, Luca. Why don't you use these rooms instead? They feel much more friendly and welcoming,' she asked as he went around the room fixing lights into more of the specially designed holders on the walls.

'I don't need places to be "friendly". And, besides, why

would I need a bridal suite?' He paused and turned to look at her. 'I am not cut out for marriage.'

She had used that jibe on him in their distant past. Now her own words were being bounced back at her. Tears stung her eyes as she looked around the room. She soon spotted another good reason why Luca wouldn't sleep here. It was decorated with dozens of cupids.

'It was a silly question, I suppose. You aren't one for all these baby dimples, that's for sure.'

'These are merely an artistic ideal, not a literal representation of what this room was expected to produce.'

Beth swung around and gaped at him. That remark and its language were totally at odds with the Luca she had always known. What she saw now was equally amazing. He was looking over the wall paintings with the air of a true connoisseur, pointing out the quality to her with one expressive hand.

Once she had got over the shock, Beth could not resist a sly dig at him.

'Careful, Luca—you're beginning to sound like my father!'

He dropped his arm, and hooked a thumb into one of the belt loops of his jeans. Her sarcasm did not bother him at all. He put his head on one side, and looked at her with an expression close to pity.

'I always take my responsibilities seriously, Beth. When I arrived here, my great-uncle's art business was failing. I was not about to sit back and watch it die. Neither was I going to let my disappointment at having to leave the army blight the rest of my life. With plenty of spare

time on my hands, I began to read. You saw the library here
earlier.'

Beth nodded. The palazzo's reading rooms held more
books than she had ever seen in one place at any one time.

'With my great-uncle always on hand, I untangled the
mysteries of art appreciation for myself. That meant I could
combine new knowledge with my organisational skills,
and propel Francesco Fine Arts into the twenty-first
century. From there it was an easy move into international
markets. I never waste my time, Beth. If I see something I
want, I go for it. In this case, the project was to make a
success of my family's business.'

'And there's no doubt at all you've succeeded.'

Beth thought back to the efficiency of his head office,
the copy of *Time* magazine, and the priceless luxury in
which he lived. She wandered over to a small side table,
made of glistening yew wood. A pretty little porcelain dish
sat on it. She picked it up, turning over the delicate, shell-
like piece in her hands. Its base was marked with cobalt-
blue crossed swords.

'You put Meissen on display in a room you never use?'

'I may not use it, but I have plenty of guests.'

Luca gave a wolfish smile. Beth guessed he meant most
of them were women.

'That makes it worse,' she muttered. Bewitched by the
room's beauty, she had hardly taken in the fine details at
first. Now she began to look at its contents more closely.
Some of her father's enthusiasm for his work had rubbed
off on her, and Beth could recognise the styles of
Chippendale and Wedgwood. There were many other exquisite pieces of furniture, glassware and porcelain that she

could not identify, but they all murmured of quality and taste. She had no doubt every item was as genuine as Luca. The things in this bedroom alone must be worth hundreds of thousands. She gave a silent whistle of amazement.

'But you're such a perfectionist, Luca. Aren't you afraid your lovely things will get broken or stolen?'

'What sort of a host would I be, if I worried about little things like that?' he said airily, strolling over to the window.

Beth watched him walk away from her. In the past, she had done it dozens of times, but always when feeling the normal fear of any soldier's partner—that he might not return to her arms. Back then, the pain had been all in her mind. Now, Luca's new coldness had stamped it all over her heart as well. She gazed at his broad back and wide shoulders. The fine designer cut of his blue silk shirt could not disguise the power of his body. Gradually, her pangs dissolved into need. This time, she was feeling the agony of a separation from him that could never be repaired.

Her anguish was so real it trembled through her body, willing her to rush up and throw herself on his mercy all over again. As she watched he put up a hand to push aside the gauzy curtains with his slender bronze fingers. She saw the contrast of his olive skin against the white net. She remembered his touch so vividly that it hurt. Thoughts of what they had shared tugged at her like stitches in a wound that would not heal. Unable to fight her desire any more, Beth felt herself drawn across the few metres separating them. Although the thick Amritsar rug muffled all sound, Luca still sensed her movements. Turning his head, he looked at her with limpid dark eyes. They told her nothing.

She was so close now she could breathe in the warm, familiar fragrance of his cologne, although the faint shadow along his jaw line showed it was hours since he had last shaved. Her whole body ached with the desperate urge to reach out and touch him—to feel his raw masculinity.

All he did was look at her, silently and steadily. It was a tigerish expression, daring her to get within his danger zone. There would be no open invitation any more. Beth had to risk making contact on instinct alone. Nervously, she raised her hand until her fingertips could no longer resist the magnetic attraction of his proud, carved cheekbones. His skin felt exactly as she remembered. As her index finger traced the slope of his jaw she felt where the smooth, flawless surface of his cheek became roughened at his beard line.

As inflexible as Sansovino's statue of Mars, Luca allowed her caress to move slowly to his hair. Hardly daring to breathe, she continued to stroke him. Her touch drifted down around his neck to the front of the plain white fabric of his shirt. All the time his unblinking stare challenged her to continue, to tempt him beyond endurance. But there was not any direct response. Finally, Beth closed her eyes. She could not carry on laying her emotions bare like this without any encouragement. Her hand faltered and fell away. She was unable to go any further, in case he rejected her.

Then she sensed a sudden darkening of the world outside. Opening her eyes again, she saw Luca had moved his hand and let the curtain fall. Now they were both completely surrounded by shadows. He stood before her in his magnificence, a coiled spring perfectly contained by his tall, lean body. The challenge of his eyes was replaced by the defiance of his stance.

'How does it feel to be denied the one thing you desire, *tesoro?*' His native language whispered into the growing darkness but the endearment could not help her. His tone had been too painful.

'Oh, Luca…it's unbearable, especially when you speak to me like that.'

Her voice was hardly strong enough to tremble the nearest candle flame, but there was no doubt Luca heard it. In response, he moved towards her until barely a dream could slip between them. Beth dropped her head, unable to stand the pain of feeling him so close, and yet so far away. And it was then that he placed a finger under her chin and lifted her head so her gaze connected with his.

He met no resistance as he took possession of her as easily as he had always done. Beth should have known what was coming next, but she was still surprised when his mouth closed over hers. His tongue penetrated her with all the fierce passion she craved. For a few moments it was as though they had never been apart. Beth could fool herself she had never said goodbye to him, on that last terrible night in Balacha.

Luca's thrusting urgency fired Beth's desperate need for him. She clung to him with urgent hands. For five years she had quashed every emotion he inspired in her. Now her feelings rushed out in a torrent of release. She fretted over his body with her lips and tongue and fingers, but as quickly as he had embraced her he stood back.

He was breathing fast; his expression was masked. Beth felt herself crumble—Luca hadn't changed at all! Despite everything, he was still, and always would be, in control. He might allow her to touch his body, but she would never reach his heart and soul. This was no bitter-sweet reconciliation between friends. All her fierce desire and need were useless in the face of his iron will. He was rejecting her as easily as he had snatched her up.

'Don't you want me after all?' she asked, wide-cyed with realisation.

His eyes narrowed. '*Want,* certainly. But you answer your own question with those two little words "after all", Beth. After all that has happened over the past few years I don't *need* you,' he said, his voice dangerous and dark.

Beth felt his scorn like a blow. She tried to take a deep, steadying breath. Seconds before, the perfume of lavender and candles had seemed so romantic. Now it seared her lungs like acid.

Luca smiled, but while his mouth might have softened, his eyes did not. He was watching her like a cat watching a mouse.

'What is the saying—"Once bitten, twice shy?" I'm surprised a clever girl like you didn't remember that, *tesoro.*'

Her hands reached out to him, but dropped to her sides before they made contact. Passion was still burning within her, but he had discarded her.

'Luca…you were enjoying yourself… The feeling wasn't only on my side, was it?'

He gave an eloquent shrug. For a few glorious seconds, they had been pressed together so tightly, the smallest movement of his body had rubbed against hers with wicked intent.

Beth lost every shred of self-respect. She had come so far she could not give up on him now.

'Luca…look at me, please! Then tell me you didn't enjoy what we were doing just then.'

Candlelight flickered in the black pools of his eyes. It was a long time before he spoke.

'I enjoyed it very much.'

He could hardly deny it. Beth had felt the unmistakable, insistent pressure of him crushing against her. But now the look on his face mocked the flames of light dancing around the room.

'If I wanted to, I could take you right here and now, Beth. But as it would mean nothing to either of us, there would be no point.'

'You don't know that.' She looked up at him with the hopeful ghost of a smile.

'I know enough. Self-knowledge is a wonderful thing, Beth. I could have you any time I wanted, but it won't be today.'

She took a step back and stared at him, confused.

'What?'

He checked the Rolex on his wrist. 'It is getting late, Beth. My pilot will take you home, before your new neighbourhood comes alive—if you know what I mean.'

Beth groaned. The fear of what might be waiting for her back at that horrible apartment squashed all her deepest physical needs in an instant.

'Don't worry. I shall tell my pilot to see you right to your door,' Luca added quickly. 'He will have instructions not to leave until you are safely inside. And remember—don't open that door to anyone overnight. Not even me.'

Especially not you, Beth thought, with a heavy sense of finality.

'Of course—but, Luca—Luca, what has happened to you?' Her words dropped like beads and rolled across the widening gap between them. 'You're as cold and uncaring as your beautiful possessions. After five years apart, I was hoping you could have found it in your heart to forgive me…'

'Why? So that we could be together again?' he replied quite reasonably, then gave her a killer blow. 'I don't think so, Beth. I think we've both come too far. The past can't be an issue for either of us any more. All I did with that little exhibition just now is to prove it to both of us.'

Pushing his hands deep into his pockets, he sauntered out of the bedroom, heading for the main door of the suite.

'And now, as you have seen everything here, I shall go and arrange for my launch to take you back home.'

The sky over the city had long ago faded from a cloudy, milky dusk into glowing velvet. It made no difference whatsoever to Luca. He remained seated beside the window of the bridal suite. He was as still as any of the marble statues guarding his piece of heaven on earth. There was a glass in his hand. Sensing trouble, his barman had mixed him a large Bellini. Luca had not touched it. The room became dark as one by one the candles around the room burned down. He did not relight them.

This was a time for shadows. Showing Beth everything she was missing had been harder than he had imagined it would be—much harder. But it was over now. Nothing would ever be so difficult for him again. He had freed her from the burden of her guilt by letting her put it into words. That should have freed him, too. Now they could both move on. Luca had faced his own demons. By putting himself to the test he knew he could resist her, though it took a huge effort. Beth now thought his love for her was dead, and he had cut her out of his life for ever with his trademark military precision.

If only he could be sure of that himself.

Self-pity wasn't in Beth's nature, but she knew the change in Luca was because of the way she had treated him in the past. Memories gnawed at her, bringing tears to her eyes. She was trying so hard not to cry she had to meet Luca's pilot with her head down. Her torment was so acute she stepped into the palazzo's speedboat without any of her usual hesitation. She had not been in Venice for long enough to use boats with the casual ease of the locals. They thought no more of travelling over water than she would of hopping into a car, but Beth was only a beginner. The pilot helped her in, before removing the waterproof cover from a seat so she had somewhere dry to sit. Tonight, she did not have the heart to enjoy the luxury of her lift home. Passengers on the waterbuses gasped and pointed as Luca's speedboat swept past them, but Beth hardly noticed. She huddled down in her jacket, going over the wrong turnings she had taken in life, and rubbing her eyes raw with the pain of rejection. Luca was the only man she wanted—now and for ever. If he didn't want *her,* then Beth's heart had no future. It was unbearably painful, but she knew she must turn her disaster into an opportunity. Now, she ought to be able to throw all her energy into making something of the rest of her life. Thoughts of Luca threatened to choke her with tears, but she refused to cry in front of his pilot. She *would* work out how to get herself back on track, if only to show Luca she didn't need him any more, or his money.

The lights of a vaporetto rose up out of the growing gloom. The glare made her blink, as though it were shining right into her murky past. Her father had managed to send her to a good school, but Beth had been more interested in making well-connected friends than in getting an education. Scraping through GCSEs and dropping out before A levels had set her up for a glittering career as a party animal. Then her father's health scares had brought a reality check. Beth had started to realise that life was about responsibilities, as well as the right to party. She had had to face facts then, and find some way of supporting her father.

Trying to find a job had given her a nasty dose of reality. Beth had discovered she was almost unemployable, despite all her contacts. Nobody would risk taking on such an airhead. She had been forced to grow up almost overnight. Staff at her local public library had given her lots of help, and she had decided voluntary work would be a good way to improve her image. As usual, she had called on a friend of a friend to provide something. This time she had got what she deserved—a position nobody else had wanted. The job of dogsbody for a charity team in a tense foreign country had felt like the world's revenge on all her time-wasting. Updating computer records, running errands, mopping up and hosing down had meant Beth was soon absorbed by eighteen-hour days. She'd had no enthusiasm left for a social life. Then Luca had arrived at the medical unit where she was working, to visit one of his men. Beth had seen him, and burst back into life.

The speedboat hit a patch of choppy water, and Beth instinctively grabbed her seat and held on. She tried to forget her wonder at meeting Luca for the first time, and to focus only on his coldly practical loan of this craft and pilot for her journey home. That was the no-nonsense Luca she had to deal with now. But his generosity kept reminding her of how things had been, once upon a time. The moment he had returned from that hospital visit in Balacha, he had sent her two dozen roses and a handwritten note thanking her for all her hard work. From then on, Beth had been entranced. Knowing Luca had made her life worthwhile again. During all their desert picnics, Beth had been too starry-eyed to wonder where the contraband champagne had come from. Today, she ran her hand idly over the smooth leather upholstery of this brand-new boat. It made her realise just how sharp the contrast was between her and Luca now. He must have as many glamorous contacts as she'd had, back in the good old days. He just didn't flaunt them.

They were approaching a jetty. Beth looked around, already nervous. The shadows were growing, and she wanted to get behind her locked door before it got any darker. As the pilot tied up and helped her ashore Beth tried to cheer herself up with thoughts of the good times. Luca was an irresistible man, and he had been an even better soldier. Dedicated to his work with the peacekeeping force in Balacha, he had always put the army first. To begin with, the little notes he had sent Beth via office captain

Tristram Anderson had been a sweet touch. And the making-up after each absence had been spectacular…

Back then, life as Luca's wife had really appealed to Beth. It had offered the dream of a lot more fun, and no swabbing of floors or sterilising instruments. The trouble was, Luca might have been romantic, but he had always made it clear his work meant more to him than marriage. He had not wanted to be tied down. The army had provided more than enough order in his life. Freedom from all other commitments had been vital for him.

Beth had been different. She had wanted a proper home, and to enjoy the kind of stability her father used to provide for her. She had craved a nine-to-five existence, with no worries about how the next supermarket shopping would be paid for. One final demand, and Luca had wrecked all her dreams. And now she was marooned in this dreary Venetian backwater.

As the pilot made Luca's boat secure Beth tried to take in her surroundings. Tenement buildings leaned over her like sea cliffs. As she was led through the lanes a million mangy cats disappeared into doorways. Luca's pilot refused her offer of coffee, and she was glad. The moment her door was locked she shut her eyes and clutched her head in lonely despair. Why, oh, why did Tristram Anderson make me tell Luca it was marriage or nothing? Because he was too spineless to make an open play for me himself, Beth thought bitterly. He wanted Luca safely out of the way before he tried anything.

Luca's friend and messenger Tristram had had a nice, respectable desk job inside the army. The closest he had got to action was writing bullet points. The only thing Beth and Luca had ever argued about was the future, and their worst fights had always happened within Tristram's earshot. They had been carried on over the phone, with Beth safe at base camp and Luca out in the field. Tristram had always been there for her in the office armed with tea, sympathy and plenty of tissues. During one explosive argument with Luca, Beth had snapped and done what Tristram had been suggesting for months. A wedding, or you can walk away, she had said.

And that had been the end of it all.

Beth's guilty conscience had plenty of company on her first night in Venice. Tap-dancing mice, paper-thin partition walls and noisy neighbours all added to her misery. Things died down around three. By that time she was so scared of sleeping through her alarm and being late for work, she could not risk staying in bed. Instead, she got up and made herself busy. Throwing herself into housework concentrated Beth's mind. She was facing a painful truth. In the split second between recognising Luca and realising his feelings for her had changed, Beth had imagined her father's voice. *Catch yourself a rich husband, and you're made for life,* it had whispered. It was a horrible reminder of the clinging parasite she had been, back in Balacha. Luca must think she was still like that, and the realisation made Beth cringe. She *had* changed. The crucible of Balacha had altered everything. Beth did not want to be dependent on others any more. It had made her vulnerable in the past, when she had thought she was safe. Once, she had made a career of relying on her so-called friends for everything. Then, snaring Luca simply for the size of his pension fund would have been totally in character for her. Now, she was determined to find her own way in life. She was proud of being such a good PA. The trouble was, Luca paid her salary now, not Ben. Unless she could persuade him she was serious about this new way of life, her time at FFA would be limited. There had to be a way of making her position more secure. She had to show Luca she could be an asset to him, and his firm, after all. The only way she could do that was to immerse herself in FFA work and absorb all she could about the business.

As she scrubbed and cleaned and rearranged her few pieces of rented furniture in the grisly flat Beth came to a decision. The next chance she got to speak to Luca alone, she would ask him what she could do to learn more.

It wouldn't be a climb-down, or a return to her bad old ways, she told herself. It was simply networking. That was what sensible people did. They used contacts to keep themselves up to date and get the best advice. She *really* needed this job. It was spectacularly good pay for someone with few qualifications and no experience, and she knew how lucky she was to have it. She needed money, and fast. There were all her father's debts to settle, and she was only managing to keep the tenancy of Rose Cottage through the generosity of her uncle, the landlord. This was the ideal situation—she would make a fresh start through work, here in Venice. And, however she might yearn, there would be no romance on the horizon—she would have to force herself to get used to that idea. However difficult it might be.

Litres of black coffee later, Beth dragged herself into

work. Then she wished she hadn't bothered. It was hell. She made a lot of silly typing mistakes, and only remembered she hadn't backed up the morning's work when she accidentally deleted a whole spreadsheet. Exasperated, she decided to go out and fetch Ben's elevenses from a deli, rather than nipping upstairs for something from the executive lounge. The fresh air would wake her up, and Luca was bound to be hard at work in his own office. In the brutal light of day, the thought of seeing him again made her uneasy about her grand plans. Pretending to care more about her work than she did about him would take an almost unbearable effort. The way she felt now, everything would probably end in tears. At least if she was careful, there was no chance of meeting him beyond the executive floors of FFA during working hours.

Or so she thought. As she hurried past a particularly smart café in a very fashionable *strada* she heard his voice.

'Elizabeth…Beth? It's not like you to be out in broad daylight. What's the matter?' His soft, beautifully accented English drifted over of the strains of the café's resident piano player.

She stopped, and had to look back to see him. Luca must have watched her pass by before deciding to speak. He was leaning against the door of the building—perfectly groomed women and paunchily prosperous men regarded him with awe as they passed on their way in, or out.

'You look like a tiger in a dogs' home,' she observed, and was rewarded with a wry smile.

'I've been hosting a business meeting here. My clients like to see me living their dream. They enjoy a little easy listening while we work, and prefer the international snacks served here, rather than the local food on offer back at FFA. You don't think I would come to a place like this voluntarily, do you? I leave that to social climbers—much like you once were.'

Beth blushed, remembering her past. 'I needed a walk,' she said cautiously. Switching her handbag to the other side, she clamped it under her arm like someone trapping a secret. 'Coming out to fetch a snack seemed ideal, but Ben is waiting. I have to hurry back.'

'Oh, let him do his own running about for once.' Luca made an expansive gesture. 'Come and have a hot chocolate, to show there are no hard feelings between us.'

Beth's face drained like a bank account. 'In a ritzy place like *that?*'

'Don't worry, I'll pay. I know how rich English families get to stay that way. They are careful never to spend their own money.' Luca rolled his eyes, but as she got close enough for him to study her properly he whistled. 'Our brand of fresh air obviously doesn't agree with you, Beth! Waiter?' He called over his shoulder into the depths of the café. 'Hold the chocolate, please; the lady will have a double espresso instead.'

'More coffee is the last thing I need today, thanks. I'm fine.' She waved away his concern. 'I didn't sleep very well last night. That's all.'

He looked intently into her face. 'It does not look as though you have slept at all.'

She shrugged. 'The amorous neighbours and the blood feuds kept me awake.' She tried to laugh at the horror of her night. 'And the assorted vermin.'

Luca reached inside his jacket and pulled out his mobile. After stabbing out a few numbers, he began speaking quickly in Italian. 'Ettore? I want you and a couple of guys to come to the office. Collect the keys to Miss Woodbury's apartment and have all her possessions brought home to the palazzo. I shall tell Silvia to put her in a guest suite. Miss Woodbury will be staying with us for a while. *Ciao!*'

He snapped the phone shut before Beth could react, but she flared up anyway.

'Now wait a minute, Luca—I'm not having strange men stripping my flat!'

'OK—so take the rest of the day off and go with them to supervise.'

'And how can I possibly move into your place, anyway? What if Ben finds out?'

Luca called for his bill. He was looking at her as though she were mad.

'It won't be a matter of finding out, because this isn't a secret. You can tell him—and anyone else who bothers to ask—the truth. They will understand. What is wrong with that? Your apartment is uninhabitable. You and I shared a...mutual friend. So I am helping you out, temporarily. Why look so shocked, Beth? That's all there is to it.'

After their confrontation of the night before Beth was painfully aware of that, but she wasn't fooled by Luca's careless manner. She had seen the way he'd grimaced when he'd referred to Tristram as their 'mutual friend' and knew exactly what must be going through his mind. Her day had started badly. If Luca was going to bring up her self-seeking past, she was on the way down to an even deeper circle of hell.

'I'd rather you said we were related!' she said with a shudder. 'With your background, it's believable. Does Ben know your mother came from London?'

'Everyone who reads the financial press must know that by now.' He finished his drink. His expression thoughtful, he said, 'There's no need for any deception in my dealings, Beth.'

His voice ran like experienced fingers up and down her spine. Combined with his smile, the effect was heavenly. But Luca was soon back to business. 'Why should Ben need to know where you live? If anyone starts asking any awkward questions, send them to me. I'll soon convince them it's nothing more than a convenient arrangement. Aren't you going to get moving? Anybody would think you were enjoying my company, Beth. You need to be back at your desk as soon as possible, in time to meet Ettore and the boys.'

Before she could get a word in edgewise, he held up his hand. 'No arguments! By moving into my palazzo you will be right on the spot for my party on Friday night. It will also mean you can be taken to work in my launch each morning. You will never be late while you are living in my house.'

She could believe it. Luca was punctual to a fault. It was Beth's fault she wasn't often punctual.

'Living in my house will be perfect for you,' he went on, warming to his idea. 'You will not have to worry about tottering through the streets, trying to get to that horrible flat on those pretty little high heels you love so much.'

'Wind back a minute—so this party you're hosting for Ben is going to be at your palazzo?'

'Of course. There could be no finer setting. And after I told my clients all about my two new employees, they cannot *wait* to be impressed by you.'

Beth gave a hollow laugh. 'You've seen the luxury in which I live right now, Luca!'

He pushed himself upright and strolled with her as they headed off. 'I'm inviting you for your beautiful English voice and your social skills, Beth, nothing more. I intend people to have a good time.' His smile was dazzling. 'And I know you'll bring your own special brand of class to the evening. It's my job as host to give people what they want. Only one thing really impresses a member of the Italian chattering class, and that's real, living members of the aristocracy. I'll have Earl Ben and his PA, who is the granddaughter of a duke, on display under my roof. They'll love it.'

Beth had been waiting for the chance to interrupt him and explain her wish to learn more about the business and maybe get more involved. Hearing that he wanted her to do nothing but impress his guests changed things. She pursed her lips and fell into step beside him. Perhaps it would be better to keep quiet about her idea, at least for the moment. Luca might think she would try and use his party just for her own selfish reasons, not for the good of FFA. If he did, she would never convince him she wanted to find her own way out of the mess she was in. She had to let him see how determined she was to succeed on her own terms. Until he had proof of that, he'd think she wanted him to bail her out. But the emotionally needy girl

Luca had rejected in Balacha was gone for ever—although he didn't know it yet.

So Beth decided to keep quiet and sit on her own ambitions, at least until his party was over.

CHAPTER FOUR

BETH travelled light. It didn't take the workmen long to pack all her belongings and ferry them over to the palazzo. Taking Luca's advice, she left Ben to fend for himself for the first time since she had taken the job as his PA, and went with them.

Thoughts of Luca had been racing through her mind all morning. The memory of his low, deep voice whispered continuously in her ears. As she stepped onto the wide pavement in front of his home she looked up at the grand west front of the building and sighed. There were three words she ached to hear him say. *I love you.* But it was an impossible dream. The looks of dark disdain he could give her now told Beth that. And he had recoiled the instant she had melted into his arms. She still winced at the pain of that rejection. But as she remembered that embrace her body reacted with a rush of adrenalin. There had *been* a reaction between them. Not even Luca could deny the insistent pressure of his arousal. The thought of it made her close her eyes and imagine…

For a few precious moments she could almost convince herself her fantasies might still come true. Then the main doors of the palazzo creaked open, and she was escorted inside.

Her surroundings helped to fan the flames of hope, if only for a few seconds. The entrance hall Beth remembered as being cold and formal was now much more welcoming. The crackle and hiss of a huge log fire brought it to life. Tall yellow flames danced in a great black hearth, outshining the glow of a dozen electric lights. As each twig caught it crackled like gunfire and sent sparks bouncing across the marble floor. Had Luca ordered it in honour of her arrival? With one look at the woman who greeted her, Beth realised it might be better if he *hadn't* made any special arrangements. Silvia, his housekeeper, did not look the sort to enjoy entertaining guests. She wore a severe black uniform and an expression to match. Too scared to smile, Beth greeted her with a formal handshake. Silvia burrowed beneath her spotless white apron and brought out a heavy iron ring noisy with keys.

'As we have no idea how long you will be here, Signorina Woodbury, I have put you in the bridal suite.' Silvia's lip curled with distaste.

Beth wondered how many of Luca's girlfriends Silvia had seen come and go. It wasn't something she wanted to know. But to judge from her expression, she might just tell me unless I can brazen this out somehow, Beth told herself.

'Thank you, Silvia, that's wonderful,' she said with a wide, innocent smile. 'When Signor Francesco showed me around, it was the part of the house I liked best.'

Silvia's face froze. I've managed to surprise her, Beth thought, and felt every muscle in her body relax a fraction.

'But those rooms are furthest away from the master suite, signorina.'

'Which suits me fine, Silvia. May I go straight up?' Beth said lightly, already heading for the stairs. 'What has Signor Francesco told you about me?'

'Nothing, as usual.' The housekeeper snorted. Beth had to laugh.

'Good, then I'll get in first with the truth, Silvia, so you can hate me for a reason rather than waiting for me to pounce on your employer. Luca and I used to be an item, a long time ago. I was young, and too stupid to know how lucky I was. I left him for another man. So I'm only here today because of his generous nature, believe me.'

The housekeeper stopped. Beth went on walking up the wide, shallow staircase, only pausing when she realised Silvia was staring at her, horrified.

'You left him? *Our signor?*'

'Yes—impossible to believe, isn't it?' Beth pouted. 'But I had my reasons at the time. I loved him, but he didn't love me as much as I thought I deserved. Luca lived for his work. That's hard to take when you are young. And when another man offers you a shoulder to cry on…'

'Pah! You are *still* young.' Silvia rustled up the stairs, passed Beth and started off along the wide, portrait-heavy landing. Luca's housekeeper was the model of efficiency again, but Beth was glad to see she no longer looked quite so bad-tempered.

All Beth's luggage had been taken up in the service lift, so she spent the next couple of hours arranging her belongings. Her suite was pure luxury. The Meissen dish and many others like it had been filled with dried rose and lavender petals, and their subtle perfumes drifted through the warm air. Although there was no one else around, the rooms were so grand Beth found herself creeping about like a mouse.

One of the first things she did was to open every window. It let in a cheerful racket from the canal below, which made her smile. As she looked down Beth saw Silvia leaving the palazzo by the front door. That was a surprise— she had assumed all the staff lived in, but Silvia was obviously off for the night. Beth wondered where she was going, and hoped it wasn't far. Mist was already beginning to drift in from the lagoon. It smudged the lights of bobbing water taxis into glowing dots, dancing like fireflies as dusk approached.

It wasn't long before Beth realized she was hungry. Her lunchtime snack had not gone very far. She should have checked with Silvia about what would be happening while she was staying at the palazzo—was she supposed to prepare her own food, or would it be provided? And she would have to ask about paying rent. Beth's spirits had been kept alive by the idea of living under the same roof as Luca. Now she began to feel uncertain again. Moving into the bridal suite was bound to be as expensive as it was luxurious. She looked around, uncomfortable at the way she had made herself at home. Perhaps she ought to go and ask in the kitchen what the arrangements were.

She didn't get that far. As she was walking down the grand staircase a member of staff was opening the doors for Luca to step in. Beth stopped, transfixed. The only man she had ever loved arrived in a billow of fog. No matter how many times she looked at him, Beth knew it could never be enough. For precious moments she feasted on the sight of him, striding into the sanctuary of his house. Her position on the stairs meant he did not see her straight away. She was able to watch him spreading out his capable hands to the warmth of the fire, which was now roaring like a furnace. It was only when the butler caught her eye that Beth managed to struggle out of her trance.

'L-Luca! I was coming down to see if there was anything I could do towards dinner.'

She reached his side as he shrugged off his coat giving Beth another excuse to watch him covertly. His sable hair was misted with droplets of water, each one alive with light from the hearth. As the fire warmed him he began to relax into something like the Luca she had once known. And yet there was something missing. The hollowness in his eyes reflected that new, strange heartlessness. And brought her up short. Thinking back, she remembered all the romance Luca used to bring to her life in the way of flowers, chocolates and midnight drives into the middle of nowhere. Could she honestly say what she felt for the man behind all those gestures was love? Had she been so infatuated back then it had made her blind to this side of him? Perhaps Luca had been hiding these same feelings beneath all his charm, back then. She nipped her lip. All she could rely on now was his generosity.

'You are a guest in my house.' Luca's voice brought her back to the present. 'The only thing I expect from guests is that they should be polite, and good company. I know you are both. That's enough for me.'

Beth clasped her hands. Although the entrance hall

could never be called 'cosy', it was warm beside the fire. It made the cold clamminess of her palms come as a shock.

'Look, I must talk to you, Luca. It's so kind of you to let me stay—'

Still looking into the depths of the fire he cut her off. 'I know what you are going to say, so I'll save you the trouble.' His smooth, lilting accent enveloped her. 'I would not dream of asking you to pay rent during your stay here, Beth. Think of it as a simple bonus. You need some kind of recognition for all the work you have to put in as Ben Simpson's PA. There's no need to hurt his feelings by telling him, though. He can think of your stay here as merely a private arrangement between…' he looked down at his hands, wriggling his cold fingers to bring back the circulation '…friends.'

His hesitation made Beth think that was the last thing they would ever be. Swallowing her disappointment, she nodded.

'That's generous of you, Luca. But you must let me do something for you in return—why don't I go and arrange dinner?'

He smiled, glancing at his watch again. 'There's no need. It must be nearly ready by now, Beth. I'm assuming you would prefer to dine in your room.'

The desire to put her arms around him and plead until he let her sit with him almost overwhelmed her, but Beth knew what she was expected to say.

'Thank you, Luca. If you are sure you won't mind very much if I left you on your own tonight?' she said slowly.

'Not at all.'

He looked relieved. Beth's heart sank. Hiding her disappointment, she went back upstairs in silence, but it was not the last she heard of Luca that night. A handwritten note was delivered just before her meal. As she opened it the faintest familiar hint of Luca's aftershave drifted out. Beth began to tingle. As she looked at the flowing handwriting she knew so well the paper trembled beneath her hands. It must be a call to join him for dinner after all. Excitement filled her with liquid warmth. In her dreams she was already running through the big old house to find him, but her fantasy was short-lived. Luca's note was cool and businesslike. It was light years away from the seduction she wanted.

Beth: my party is to be a masked ball. You may wish to visit Beccas near the Rialto tomorrow, to pick up a costume. Charge anything you like to my account there—and don't worry, Ben will be given exactly the same instructions. Costumes are always provided for new members of staff. I don't expect them, or those on limited contracts, to pay for such luxuries themselves.

Beth folded the sheet of handmade notepaper and slid it back into its tissue-lined envelope. This time, Luca had made a point of mentioning her temporary status with his firm. That's to underline how little he thinks of my feelings, and me, she thought. Standing up, she went over to the fire burning in the hearth of her reception room. She ought to throw his message away. It was just a note, after all. She should drop it into the flames without a second thought.

But the fragrance of him haunted her again. She walked back to her seat at the dining table, the note still in her hand.

Next day, Beth spent the whole of her lunch hour at Beccas. The experience took her back to a time when she could afford to shop without limit, and it was lovely. She made the most of every second. At the mention of Luca's name, the staff lost their haughty looks and treated her like a princess. She was settled in a soft, comfortable armchair with a large latte. All she had to do was relax, while they hurried upstairs and down, bringing beautiful gowns for her to look at. Soon she was surrounded by a collection of sumptuous dresses in sensual brocades, lace, and velvet in jewel-like colours. Everything was perfumed with expense and sleek with extravagance. It was like the old days. Beth was so happy; she could not resist taking Luca at his word. She did not ask the price of anything, but this time it wasn't because she didn't care. It was because she was afraid of losing her nerve. For years, she had been counting every single penny she spent. She had developed an allergy to large bills, and wasn't going to risk it flaring up with an attack of guilt. I'm only following Luca's instruction, she kept reminding herself, and ordered on. She took her time, choosing exactly what she wanted right down to the finishing touches of hat, bag and full-length evening gloves.

It was luxury to give instructions for the bill to be delivered to the palazzo, along with her parcels. And then a little china clock in the changing room discreetly chimed the hour, and she jumped like Cinderella. It's time to go back to the real world, she thought with a sigh. People who gave a palazzo as their address shouldn't have to worry about little details like time, but Beth was an employee as well as a guest. She finished her shopping, and said goodbye to the staff with a heavy heart.

It was only when she was safely out of their sight around a corner she could break into a run, desperate to get back to work on time.

Beth did not see Luca all day. He had left early for work and stayed late. It gave her no opportunity to thank him, or tell him about the things she had bought. She had to hug her excitement to herself until she got back to the bridal suite that afternoon. It was worth the wait. A magnificent selection of silver boxes were neatly stacked on the table of her reception room. They begged to be torn open and enjoyed. It took all Beth's will-power to walk straight past and head for the bathroom, but getting ready was a treat in itself. The huge copper bath took ages to fill, and the sensation of sinking neck-deep in rose-scented bubbles was indescribable. She sighed again at how lucky Luca was. His palazzo combined all the gracious living of days gone by, with every modern luxury. Its painted ceiling was protected from the steamy atmosphere by specially designed glazing, allowing Beth to admire it without being troubled by reflections. She lay back, soaking away the strains of the day to the soft sounds of Mozart. The music was being discreetly piped through from a sophisticated audiovisual control centre in her living room. When she stepped out of the bath, her feet sank into a floor covering as thick and soft as the specially warmed towels laid out ready for her. Simply relaxing in Luca's house was beyond wonderful. She could hardly wait to find out what sort of parties he held.

Naked except for a towel around her freshly washed hair, Beth padded through the suite to fetch her prizes. She laid all the boxes out on her bed, and then stood back—but only for a second. The temptation was too much. Snatching at the pink ribbons tied around each parcel, she sent silver wrapping and tissue paper flying as she delved into box after box. Evening gloves, a mask and her hat were discovered and wondered at before she reached the greatest treat of all. She opened the largest parcel with great care, like the stellar present it was.

'I knew it was beautiful, but I'd forgotten just how lovely it was!' She breathed, stirring the rustling folds of tissue. Inside the box lay a full-length velvet gown, in a shade of blue exactly matching her eyes. The dress was lined with satin, and Beth needed both hands to lift it from its soft, luxurious bed. The bodice was heavily boned and designed to make the most of her waist, hips and breasts. Beth gulped. The neckline had not seemed *that* low in the shop. Thank goodness she would be able to hide her blushes behind a mask!

She checked the clock, and realised she should not have spent so much time in the bath. Quickly, she picked up the new underwear Luca's generosity had brought her. It was then she began having second thoughts. She had been carried away by the excitement of her shopping expedition, and this had been an extravagant mistake. Luca could never resist the rustling promise of silk and stockings, so she had treated herself. Looking at the froth of lacy underwear now, she knew it had been a waste of his money. In the old days he had always loved seeing her wear things like this. What were the chances of him experiencing any of it tonight?

Feeling a tremor of uncertainty, she looked at herself in the mirror. Her reflection stared back, the same as ever. All the changes I've made are on the inside, she thought. They're hidden away, just like this lovely lace and silk will be. Luca will never allow himself to enjoy any of it now. So much has happened since we were happy together. I'm ruined, while his career has gone into orbit. Though it obviously hasn't made him happy. I can see that every time I look into his face. If only I could find some way to ease his pain and bring a smile back to his face...

She put on the beautiful underwear as one tiny act of defiance against her heartache. Despite the fact it would be hidden, her spirits rose straight away. At least *I* shall know I'm wearing it, she thought. Then she dried her curtain of honey-blonde hair and stepped into her gown. The friction of new silk underwear against her skin had been wonderful, but it was nothing compared with the heavy luxury of her dress. Beth rose to the occasion. She felt like a million dollars. The moment was only broken when she caught sight of herself in the mirror again, and saw her bra would have to go. Straps were not an option in an evening gown like this. Removing it, she had to admire the way the bodice fitted her like a second skin. It supported and enhanced her natural curves until she billowed like a Renaissance goddess.

This is dressing-up as an art form, Beth thought as she added accessories one by one. White silk evening gloves and matching court shoes meant she was covered from head to foot, apart from that tantalising amount of cleavage. The Venetian obsession with masquerades meant the costumiers had thought of everything. Beth's outfit even included a wig. With great care, she arranged its tumble of luxurious auburn curls over her own straight hair. As a last touch she added an airy coronet of stripped feathers and net, which had been dyed to match her dress. The effect was ravishing. Not even Luca would recognise her tonight—and in the security of her own room Beth wondered if it might give her the break she needed.

Behind this disguise, anything might be possible. She cross-examined her mirror, but it did not reflect her expression. The white mask she was wearing kept its Mona Lisa smile, whatever worries tortured her beneath the surface.

A table had been set up in the grand marble entrance hall. It was covered with a floor-length damask cloth, and silver urns packed with bottles of champagne on ice. Behind it, waiters stood in readiness, immaculate in white jackets and black ties. They were getting some last-minute instructions from a tall figure in a full-length black cape, lined with blood-red satin. A silver mask dangled from his fingers as he pointed out details. No disguise would have hidden his identity from Beth. It was Luca. There was no mistaking him, even when he had his back to her. She caught her breath. He looked magnificent, so she stopped on the stairs and enjoyed watching him for a few seconds. Feeling her gaze, he turned around. His face was dark and serious—but then he saw her.

'Don't move.'

The way he was looking at her drew Beth like a magnet.

It was hypnotic. She had to disobey—there was no choice. Her body made her take two more steps—not downwards, but towards the stone balustrade. She leaned over, held by the look in his eyes.

'You look…ravishing, Beth.'

'I'm supposed to be in disguise,' she began, but he shook his head.

'I would have recognised you anywhere.'

His appreciative eyes made up for everything. All her fears and worry vanished as she descended the stairs in a swish of heavy velvet skirts. He watched her all the way across the hall. As she reached him the corners of his lips lifted momentarily in a smile.

'We have your favourite pink champagne, Beth.' Although he kept his voice low, the rich tones of his accent echoed around the great hall. Opening the bottle himself, he poured out a slender glass and held it up to her.

'Nobody was supposed to know it was me under this disguise.' She sighed, accepting the drink from him. 'I thought the whole idea of these masked balls was mystery.'

He dipped his head and whispered, 'You will always be an enigma to me, Beth.' Then, pouring himself half a glass of champagne, he touched it lightly to hers. The crystal rang with the same perfect pitch of excitement that was vibrating down Beth's spine. His eyes had softened, encouraging her to go further than she thought possible.

'It doesn't have to be like this,' she began in a low voice.

He watched her for a moment and then he smiled a dark, mesmerizing smile. Those beautiful long, dark lashes lifted as the light in his eyes began to dance in the way she had missed for so long. And as his hand began to rise slowly from his side she knew exactly what was going to happen. He was going to cup the side of her face with his long, strong fingers and raise it for a kiss. Closing her eyes, she waited, but just as he brushed her skin the hall erupted in chaos.

'Not *another* conquest, Luca!' a woman's voice drawled as guests swirled around them like floodwater. Everyone laughed—except Beth. Two, three, four people pushed between her and Luca. She let them do it. Her moment had gone. Luca might be pretending to give her soft glances over the heads of the new arrivals, but Beth could see the truth all too clearly. He had two reputations to keep up, and she wasn't part of either of them. As a serial womaniser and dedicated businessman, he was never going to push his guests aside to make a special space for her.

Crushed, she retreated from this new life he had made for himself. She could see, as he put clients and possible investors at their ease, Luca was working hard this evening. He might as well have been sitting behind a desk. He wasn't the man she had known in Balacha any more. Her hard-bitten soldier had been transformed into a sophisticated host. It was a shock. Trying to come to terms with it, she let the growing crowd carry her away from him and into the palazzo's grand ballroom.

Although her feelings were in turmoil over Luca, Beth could not help but notice the gasps of amazement as she crossed the threshold. The ballroom was a perfect fairy-tale setting for a masquerade party. Everyone was impressed. It was the largest salon in the building. Four huge crystal chandeliers, shimmering with candles, hung from the ceiling, which was a work of art in itself. Centuries before, a genius had painted it with scenes from Ancient Rome. Faded figures feasted overhead, their tables overflowing with wine, fruit and flowers. Luca's party reflected those scenes.

Every horizontal surface in the room was rich with food, champagne and exotic flower arrangements. Swags of orchids cascaded from pedestals, and crowned Luca's proud ancestors. Tables covered with gold plates of canapés were set up across one end of the room. Beth wandered over to them, drawn towards an enormous central arrangement of strelitzias and proteas. Silvia the housekeeper had already told her some of the flowers were being specially flown in from South Africa, along with their florist. Beth could not believe such extravagance. She was still more amazed to discover the flower arrangement hid a bubbling fountain. As she drew nearer a waiter in crisp white jacket and gloves ladled a glass of liquid from its pool and handed it to one of the guests. The fountain was rushing with pure champagne.

No wonder everyone looks so happy, Beth thought, and then noticed many of the smiles were directed towards her.

She sipped her drink, and tried to smile back. Her heart might be bruised and battered, but all those appreciative looks began to steady her nerves. The glass of champagne helped, too. She almost began to look forward to the evening. The only problem was Luca. She knew each time their eyes met across the crowded room, she would melt. This new Luca would see that as his right. Just the thought of trying to make a more personal approach made her shiver.

She walked around the ballroom, trying to take in her

beautiful surroundings. It was no good. Everything reminded her of Luca. It all came back to him. He had been generous enough to move her into his home, but that was just his way. It didn't mean anything. She ought to be able to treat it as nothing more than a kind gesture. But this was such a romantic setting… Seeing the pain always present in Luca's eyes these days made her long to reach out to him, but she dared not do it. He'd changed. And if Beth gave in to the urge to try and transform him again, she would lose him a second time…

Hundreds of people had accepted Luca's invitation to party. The enormous ballroom shimmered with opulent outfits. Conversation flowed as easily as the champagne. To one side, an orchestra played softly as the guests arrived. Soon, everyone was mingling. At first Beth hid behind her mask, but soon she couldn't resist joining in. Taking off her mask made talking easier, but meant she could not watch for Luca. Her interest would have been too obvious. She had to listen for his beautiful voice instead, or try to catch the lilt of his distinctive aftershave on the warmed evening air.

Beth was grabbed by a desperate need to watch him for as long as possible, and, to her amazement, it was easy. Luca was absorbed in his work as host. He looked far too busy to notice her. Here was a man who claimed to hate small talk, working his party like an expert. He was chatting, smiling and circulating as though born to it. Beth could not take her eyes off him. All the familiar feelings of longing warmed her body with a rising fever. If only she could go up and claim him, and push her hands through the dark luxuriance of his hair, surely he'd have to respond by pulling her into one of his all-consuming kisses…

'Are you all right, Beth?' Andria's voice bounced her back to reality.

'Y-yes…I'm just feeling the heat, that's all.'

'Oh, well, that's soon fixed! You'll need some Dutch courage. Especially as I've been sent over to start introducing you to everyone!' Andria giggled, hailing a passing waiter.

'No more champagne for me, thanks.' Beth shook her head and handed her crystal flute to the man. When he offered her some freshly squeezed orange juice instead, she accepted with relief. She needed something to cool her nerves as Andria began leading her through the hordes of partygoers. As group after group of strangers greeted her, Beth heard things about Luca that only made her yearning more acute. Whenever a waiter arrived to top up their drinks or offer canapés, someone in the crowd would joke, 'There's always plenty more where that came from!' It didn't take her long to realise Luca was famous for his lavish entertaining.

When they discovered Beth was not one of his latest conquests, the guests relaxed enough to laugh about the way he had a different girl for every occasion. They all agreed he showed the proper billionaire spirit, but Beth wasn't so sure. Luca had always been generous, but she'd never known him to be wasteful. Privately, she wondered if he had started using money to dull the anger that was so obviously working away inside him. Their lives might have taken totally different tracks, but Beth couldn't help wondering if Luca would eventually wind up as lonely as she was.

The orchestra launched into a series of show tunes, and

a few couples moved onto the dance floor. Beth accepted several masked partners, but none of them could ignite the rush of excitement Luca always stirred in her. She was escorted to the buffet, or chatted pleasantly with anyone and everyone, but her heart was elsewhere. All the time she was listening for the sound of Luca's voice. Whenever she thought her latest partner would not notice, she scanned the crowd trying to catch sight of him. All she saw was a glimpse of his broad back, or finely chiselled profile as he bent to listen to one of his guests. Once or twice she felt he was near, but the crowd always swirled between them. Knowing he was near but invisible fed her simmering need for him. It was so unfair. He was physically close to her, yet emotionally they were far apart...

The room grew hotter. Beth felt less and less like dancing, but the men grew merrier. When one man with large sweaty paws tried too hard to persuade her, Beth jerked back, colliding with a couple who were standing at the edge of the dance floor. There was a confusion of spilled champagne, canapé crumbs and laughing. Beth was horrified, especially when the man who had been so keen to dance with her pulled out a large white handkerchief. He started to dab at the splashes of champagne on her bodice. Hot with embarrassment, Beth looked around for rescue. It arrived. The crowds parted, and the masked but unmistakable figure of Luca swept toward her.

CHAPTER FIVE

PULLING off his mask, Luca stared accusingly at the crowd around Beth.

He said something in Italian and the crowd dispersed. His accent was harsh, and he motioned for a waiter to take her glass. Beth hung onto it defiantly. His dark eyes dared her to resist as both his hands clamped over hers. Beth knew his touch would trap her, but it was still a shock to feel all her resistance drain away. She could do nothing but watch as he lifted the glass of orange juice from her fingers, then replaced it with a full one from the tray.

'I'm sorry. I seem to have frightened your new friend Giulio away.'

Beth flushed, resenting the suggestion she could be interested in anyone but him. 'I was trying to get rid of him myself, actually.'

'My arrival seems to have done the job for you.' Luca nodded with satisfaction. 'So you can relax, Beth. There's no reason to breathe *quite* so fast now.'

She looked down. Her breasts were rising and falling rapidly, fluttering above the tightly boned bodice of her dress. She became aware that the pressure of it against her nipples was caressing them into peaks of excitement. Combined with the nearness of Luca, it made her temperature shoot off the scale. To try and hide the tell-tale signs of her arousal she clasped both hands around her glass and held it up to her chest. Luca responded with a hint of his old amusement.

'You're looking warm, too. Some of the other girls have brought fans. Shall I ask around and see if I can borrow one for you?'

Beth thought she saw the darkness fade from his eyes for a second as he looked at her. Then the spell was broken, and he turned away to signal for more ice. When it arrived, he picked up one of the glittering cubes with a pair of silver tongs.

'How many?' He hovered it over her new glass of juice. 'Just one? Or—'

A freezing droplet of water fell straight down into her cleavage. With a squeal of surprise Beth clapped one hand to her mouth. She looked around guiltily, but hardly anyone had noticed, and only one person cared.

Luca was laughing. *Really* laughing!

'Do you remember the time when—?' he began, but as the ice hit her drink the temperature plummeted again. 'No…no, we mustn't start going over old ground like that.'

The usual guarded look slipped back over his face, hiding his feelings like a cloud. You don't need that silver mask to complete your disguise, Beth thought. Your features are set in one for most of the time. Thanking him for the ice, she tried to think of some way to bring the long-lost smile back to his face again.

'Will the two of us be eating our way through leftover

party food for breakfast tomorrow, Luca?' She laughed softly.

He looked around the crowd, and almost stopped frowning. 'There won't *be* any leftovers. This lot are worse than locusts. It's the same at all my parties—I want my guests to be able to indulge.'

It was then she saw the first hint of a smile from Luca. 'It pleases them. And seeing people enjoy themselves pleases me. Which reminds me—why didn't you make your customary grand entrance to the party, Beth? When I looked around you were edging your way in here like a little mouse. It isn't like you to pass up the chance of being the centre of attention.'

She smiled nervously, fluttering her fingers around the rim of her glass. 'I don't really know anyone in Venice yet, except you and Ben.'

'All the more reason to make a statement, I would have thought.' His voice became low and teasing, and what happened next almost stopped Beth's heart. Taking the glass of orange juice out of her hands, he lodged it on the nearest table. Then he reached for her arm and looped it into the crook of his elbow. In an instant she went from being a lost soul to being held firm against the warm stability of him.

'Come with me to the orchestra platform, Beth. It's time for my two new members of staff to be introduced to everyone.'

Beth could hardly take in what he was saying. It was difficult enough to believe what was happening, but the effects convinced her. Luca's appreciation always transformed her. Tonight was no exception. His magic worked instantly. As he swept her across the room on his arm she felt taller, lighter, and somehow more beautiful. The crowd ebbed away before them like a sea; with the rustle of beautiful costumes and whispers of *'Who is she?'* echoing in waves through the ballroom.

With Luca's reputation, Beth knew the question must be asked every night of the week. Escorting her like this could mean nothing to him, but for her it was priceless. For a few glorious seconds, *she* had all his attention. Right now, nothing else mattered.

On their way across the dance floor, Luca made a small movement of his hand to summon Ben. He fell in behind his boss like the dutiful employee he was.

'Pull your mask down if you're going to laugh, Beth,' Luca whispered with a twinkle. 'The old Venetians knew what they were doing when they perfected the masquerade. It gives everyone the chance to hide their real feelings.'

He was right. All sorts of intrigues could be carried on behind masks. Romances might start and secrets could be passed, all behind a veil of respectability. No names, no pack drill, was the phrase Luca used. Beth had been right to think it was a shame he had seen straight through her disguise. Anonymity might have given her the nerve to ask him for some advice.

Beth so desperately needed Luca's support. He had the experience of turning a bad situation to his own advantage. That was exactly what she wanted to do, but she was afraid. The thought of seeing his haunted, beautiful eyes harden if she asked for his help meant she could never come straight out with a request. During the evening, she had watched him talk so easily with his other masked guests.

If only she could have asked him for advice anonymously…

She stood and listened while Luca said how delighted he was to welcome his two new employees. Most of his praise was directed towards Ben. In the past, Beth would have complained at being sidelined. Tonight she was relieved Luca glossed over her arrival, as there were many important sponsors in the audience. They didn't need reminding that the wages of Ben's pet PA would be coming out of the company's profits. I don't want to be a parasite any more, Beth thought. The sooner I can strike out on my own, the better. She had grown to hate relying on other people. Asking Luca for help in finding a new career would be the last time she used anyone—if only she could find the courage to take that first step.

When Luca's announcement had been made, Ben thanked him on behalf of himself and Beth. With relief, she realised this meant she didn't need to say anything, just lap up the praise. The whole, vast room applauded them. Then Luca announced the music would begin again.

'Thank you,' Luca nodded to Ben and Beth in turn. 'And now, I promised the next dance to the Austrian minister's wife. If you would both excuse me…'

Treating them to his usual professional smile, Luca swept off without a backward glance at Beth.

'Luca, wait!' Beth called, but he did not seem to hear her. She stared after him in bewilderment. Were things so bad between them he only paid attention to her when she could be useful to his image?

Men immediately surrounded Beth, all asking her to dance. She accepted several offers one after another, but it was only to keep Luca's show on the road. He wanted his guests to have a happy evening. Dancing with some of them was the least she could do to help him, but none of them made any impression on her. Luca was the only partner she wanted, but it was a hopeless dream. He kept himself fully occupied with everyone else. She didn't want to notice, but, as always, Luca was impossible to ignore. He had become a chameleon, forever changing according to his surroundings. And his surroundings were now out of this world, Beth thought, looking around at the happy, well-fed guests enjoying his opulent palazzo. Luca had adapted, and spectacularly. Somehow, she was going to have to do the same.

At one o'clock in the morning, a ball supper was announced. Cocktails were mixed by a flock of uniformed staff. Silver dishes of seafood snacks were handed around, and every variation on the theme of coffee was on offer. Beth was looking forward to a rest, but she didn't get one. One minute she was trying to find a place to park her empty glass. The next second Luca was standing in front of her: tall, broad and wearing what he used as a smile nowadays.

'I knew I could rely on you to make a good impression tonight, Beth.'

She was not fooled for one second. 'Hmm…I can hear a "but" hovering in your voice, Luca.'

'Some of the men who work for me have what you might call—' he raised his shoulders and spread his hands '—elastic morals?'

'Well, you're a fine pot to be calling kettles black!'

He looked at his watch, and his smile faded. 'Yes, but I can look after myself, Beth. I came over to give you some advice. Try and keep your distance from my male guests. They aren't all to be trusted when it comes to a beautiful woman in such a stunning outfit. Especially Giulio Rosso…there is a rumour going around he wants to set up in business on his own account, hoping to use contacts he has made while working for FFA.' Luca spoke as though it was an unforgivable sin.

'Oh…' Beth nipped her lip.

He saw the gesture and looked concerned. 'You're worried, I can tell. What is it, Beth?'

She had been screwing up her courage all evening. It had reached a point where she was almost ready to ask Luca for help and to hell with the consequences. Now he was telling her he hated people who used contacts they made through him. How could she try and take advantage of his knowledge after a warning like that?

'I—I'm sorry, Luca. I've had to promise Giulio the next dance, in return for a few minutes' peace now.'

Luca looked around like a hawk at the chattering crowds.

'So where is he now, then, this latest conquest of yours?'

'He's gone to fetch me a coffee.'

Luca raised his brows in mock irritation and summoned a waiter. 'You don't need to change the habits of a lifetime, Beth. A night like this calls for more.'

Beth thanked the waiter, but refused a drink from his tray of sparkling cocktails.

'Quite honestly I was glad of an excuse to send Signor Rosso off for refreshments, Luca. He seems the sort who might easily get distracted by someone else on the way. I was hoping he'd never make it back to me.'

Luca was about to pick up a glass from the cocktail tray but when he heard that, he abandoned it.

'Damn it—forget him, forget all this and dance with me instead. I can show you that although I may have gone too far last night, it was an exception,' he added, with an unusually mischievous twinkle.

Beth hesitated. All she wanted was to feel Luca's arms around her again. Perhaps the tiny thaw she had noticed when he had added ice to her drink was still going on. She hadn't seen him look this relaxed since her arrival in Venice.

He raised a brow and smiled wickedly. 'And, anyway, a good host will always please his guests.'

Beth's dream of rekindling their romance faltered and died. She ought to have guessed that asking her to dance was nothing but a gesture to him. Why can't he see it means so much more to me? she thought desperately. Too scared to speak in case she said something silly the moment he touched her, Beth looked up at him. Luca was already tired of waiting. Putting out his hand, he took hers, crushing her soft skin in the sandpaper grip she knew so well. His other hand slid around her waist and drew her in towards his body. Suddenly, words were no longer a problem because nothing could express the way Beth felt. The only thing that mattered was the certainty of his hands. He guided her into the dance. She was speechless with delight at the way he took control, holding her close and sweeping her around the floor.

'You can stop looking so surprised, Beth. It's only a

waltz, after all.' He looked down at her expectantly as they circled the room together.

Despite her breathless panic, she managed to mumble something in reply. His smile widened.

'It's a vital skill for an officer, Beth. As you would have known if you had bothered to ask me, once upon a time.'

Beth flushed. 'But you would never take me to formal dances!' she managed to say. 'That was why I accepted Tristram's first invitation, and all the trouble started. He was your friend, and I thought he was only being friendly to me in turn. By the time I realised he had more in mind, it was too late.'

Luca's snort of derision brought her back to earth. His disbelief stung, and in seconds all the disappointment and rage she had stifled over the years came flooding back. She planted her feet down firmly in the middle of the dance floor and stopped, which meant Luca had to stop, too.

'I was lonely, Luca!'

'I hope you aren't trying to shift the blame for what happened onto me, Beth. It was your decision to finish our affair.'

'Tristram only asked me out in the first place because he felt sorry for me.'

Luca's face changed. She had shocked him, and it was a second or so before he managed to put it into words.

'And you went with him, despite the fact he pitied you?' he said incredulously.

'But I didn't know that at the time! It only came out after we—when he and I…' Beth faltered, trying not to notice all the other dancers circling around them. Every other couple was busily trying to ignore the fact their host and his partner were facing up to each other in the centre of the floor.

'You're telling me Anderson threw that accusation back at you after the event?' Luca grimaced. 'That isn't the way to treat a lady.'

Beth could hardly believe what she was hearing. 'You didn't do much better! *You* were the one who put me in that position in the first place!' she cried softly, desperate not to draw any more attention to their argument. 'You left me on my own *all* the time! You were never there! I'm not a nun, Luca.'

'Of course you aren't. Then, as now, you were always a real little *principessa.*'

It was a jibe that angered Beth, and Luca knew it. Without giving her a chance to come back at him, he swept her off her feet and back into the dance. Spinning her into a series of elaborate turns, he forced her to concentrate on her footwork. The applause at this display stopped Beth from retaliating, and gave Luca the chance to air a theory he'd been working on for a long time.

'I was "never there", Beth, because I was always so busy with the "active" part of active service. Tristram Anderson did nothing more dangerous than office work. That must have made him feel inferior. So he tried to steal you, as a way to get back at me.' His grip tightened on her fingers, but the band was reaching its finale. To applaud them, Luca dropped her hand like a red-hot ember and stood back from her. Beth studied his face as everyone clapped. He was smiling, but at his other guests—not at her.

Strolling off to the stage, Luca brought the evening to a close. Beth stood and watched him, her mind and body in turmoil. He had held her so close during their dance that for a second or two anything seemed possible. But that was over now. She felt confused and angry, as though she had woken up too soon and seen a wonderful dream snatched away from her. Luca was so handsome, so capable and once upon a time he had been hers. But she had thrown it all away.

I must have been out of my mind, she thought. Silvia the housekeeper was right—it was madness to walk away from a man like Luca. The audience here tonight was practically in love with him. You could see it in their eyes. His easy manner and beautiful speaking voice charmed them all over again as he wished them goodbye. Anyone would be insane to turn their back on him.

And I was, she thought sadly as she joined in the final applause.

Beth took advantage of the gaggle of people flocking out of the grand entrance hall to slip away unnoticed. She went straight up to her rooms. Locking the door of the suite behind her, she fell back against its solidity and stood there for a long time. She was filled with a strange mixture of relief and gloom. In the short time she had been in Venice she had come close to making a fool of herself half a dozen times. Luckily—although it hardly felt like that to Beth— Luca's attitude had always managed to stop her going the whole way, in any sense of the word. Every time she seemed to be making progress with him, he raised his defences and shut her out. If she could only make him realise she wasn't the flighty party girl he'd once known. She had done a lot of growing up, but was it enough? Until a few hours ago, Beth had convinced herself all she needed from Luca was the chance of a career. Dancing with him had scattered all her grand plans like gold dust. The touch of his hands had brought all her deepest emotions back to the surface. All she really wanted was Luca, but that fairy tale had no hope of coming true.

She flicked on a light switch. Its dazzle sparkled over the sequinned evening bag she had decided against taking to the party. Walking over to the table, she picked it up. In the silence of her lonely suite she heard a few forgotten coins roll from one end of the purse to the other. It gave her an idea. Taking out the handful of change, she dropped the bag and let herself out onto the landing again. Looking to left and right, she decided it was safe to make a quick trip downstairs. There was no one to see where she was going. Apart from the sound of cleaning staff clattering away in the ballroom, the whole house seemed deserted.

Lifting her heavy velvet skirts, she ran down the stairs and into the central courtyard. Cold moonlight fell in pools on the ancient herringbone brickwork. The wellhead cast a big black shadow over the narrow staircase leading to the upper floor, but there was enough light for Beth to see what she was doing. Stepping up onto the plinth, she clutched the coins she had brought until their metal forged new creases in her hand. Squeezing her eyes tightly closed, she made a heartfelt, desperate wish and threw her money into the blackness of the well. As the hailstorm of coins rattled against the brickwork, Beth heard a slight rustle behind her. A frisson of fear ran up and down her spine and she turned. At the exact moment her offering splashed into the invisible water far below Luca stepped out of the shadows.

CHAPTER SIX

BETH pressed one hand to the pounding pulse in her throat.

'So this well *is* magic.'

Luca shrugged. 'I was passing through.'

'Don't say you came here to make a wish, too?' Beth tried to laugh, but found she could not make any sound at all. He said nothing. Instead he prowled around the well until he was standing right beside her. The nearness of him forced words from her with the desperation of a woman drowning in guilt.

'I—I found some loose change. There's no point in keeping it rattling around—all it was doing was rubbing holes in the lining of my purse,' she gabbled, nervously running her hands up and down her arms.

'You look cold, Beth.'

She stopped. A shaft of moonlight glittered over his dark hair and made his sad, sweet smile look almost perfect. It twisted her heart until she had to look away.

'I'm all right.'

'No, you aren't.'

His fingers slipped gently beneath her chin. Turning

her head until she had to face him again, he gazed into her soul.

'I shouldn't have brought all those old frustrations to the surface again. I'm sorry.'

'You don't need to apologise for anything, Luca.' Beth sighed. 'I was a stupid fool.'

'No. You *were* misguided, though. Were you wrong to leave me? Of course.' He allowed himself a small chuckle, but it faded into silence long before his final words. 'But *never* call yourself stupid.'

He moved closer to her and Beth found herself enfolded by his warmth, wrapped up in his arms and intoxicated by the fragrance of him.

'You were spectacular this evening,' he breathed, 'but then you always were. Why do I try and fool myself?'

Beth's hands went to his chest, her fingers spreading over the fine fabric of his shirt like a plea. She could feel his lightest breath whispering over her hair, running over her skin until she was delirious with possibilities. But what could she do? Whenever she tried to reach out to him now, he rejected her. Despite his words, she could not bring herself to try again. Her head sank. Disappointment was already shining behind her eyes and she did not want him to see it.

'Beth?'

Luca spoke her name softly. She trembled. He was holding her close to his body, and must have felt her move. When his fingers traced their way around the heart-shaped outline of her face, she looked up. Tears were threatening to fill her eyes, but before she could apologise for it he kissed her.

In an instant, all her fear and pain slipped away. Desire filled the void he had left in her body. The warmth of longing infused her. It was such a long time since he had held her with genuine passion like this. She relaxed, savouring every second of the experience. She was in Luca's arms. Nothing could hurt her when life was as good as this.

For long moments he held her as though she were a piece of fine porcelain, cradling her body with the greatest care. Luca's mind was as finely tuned as a set of balance scales. Right now, he was weighing up his options. Pure chance had led to him taking this short cut to his suite at the same time Beth came downstairs. Approaching her had been a gamble. He could have remained hidden in the shadows, keeping his presence a secret. But spying on a woman was not his style. He had to do the right thing, and let her know he was there. And now this…

The past taunted him. They had been here before, so often. Whatever the crisis, whatever the argument, Beth always managed to worm her way back in. She was at work now, beneath his fingertips, but Luca was not going through that again. Beth had almost managed to ensnare him, that last night in Balacha, but he had called her bluff. He wouldn't let her invade his spirit a second time. Life ran on Luca's terms now, and he was determined to keep a tight rein on this situation.

He ran his hands over the bodice of her dress. All the fine velvet and corsetry in the world could not disguise the delicate framework it held. It can't hide the points of her nipples either, he thought, feeling a surge of testosterone as he remembered the silhouette she had made as he had watched her from the shadows. A man would have to be carved from stone to resist such temptation. Luca was all male, and he never missed an opportunity to prove it. One kiss is nothing, he told himself.

'Luca…does this mean…?' Beth breathed as he drew back from her.

He was crushing her so tightly to his body she could barely get the words out.

'Could there be another chance for us?' she managed to say.

He was looking down as though he could devour her, body and soul; he held her for an eternity. His fingers dug into her back in an agony of possession. And then he spoke.

'I've told you before, Beth. I don't need complications in my life. I have too much authority and too many responsibilities already. From now on, I'm only interested in independence. But as for this…'

He robbed another kiss from her. It left her breathless and weak, desperate for more. Feeling the effect he was having on her, Luca pulled away. Beth felt the agony of rejection all over again. Unless she managed to make something out of this situation, she would lose him for ever. If she couldn't, she would sink beneath the weight of her guilt and loss and there would be no escape. Her hold on him tightened, but this time her need for support was completely physical. She clung to him because her legs could no longer support her. All she wanted was for Luca to sweep her into his arms and carry her off. She would do anything, go anywhere he wanted if *only* she could have the chance to show him how much she needed him.

His kisses moved from her lips to her nose, and then to her forehead. Beth relaxed totally into his arms and was taken up into heaven. Luca caressed the silken sheen of her hair with his cheek, while the fingers of one hand worked through its thickness with a relish she could sense and appreciate. She had thought dancing with him was wonderful. This was infinitely better. It was heavenly beyond her wildest dreams. She wasn't going to do anything to burst the bubble of her happiness. If it meant she had to stand here until the end of time, she was more than happy.

It didn't take that long.

'Why don't we continue this conversation somewhere more comfortable?' he breathed. The words whispered as softly as a sigh through the darkness. Her heart was too full for her to reply. It was impossible to put into words what she felt so she nodded.

He savoured the moment for a long time. Then both his hands went to her hair. He stroked it gently, before moving over her shoulders. She shivered again, but this time it was with anticipation. His fingers continued their journey over the fine fabric of her dress. Reaching her waist, he encircled it with one arm, and then drew her towards the stone staircase leading to the second floor of the palazzo.

Beth walked up the steps in a dream. Leaning against him, she watched the toes of her shining satin court shoes flickering in the blue-white moonlight.

'This is like the old days,' he murmured.

Beth giggled. 'Hardly…! We're not in the middle of a war zone.'

'No, but I spent the evening watching you enjoy yourself. You were a credit to the firm tonight, *cara*.'

That single word wasn't much, but Beth knew it was something she could build on.

'It was my pleasure. Luca, you can always count on me if there's anything I can do to help FFA become more successful.'

He placed a kiss on the crown of her head. His lips lingered, and Beth knew he was revelling in the fragrance of her hair again. As they reached the landing he stopped.

'This takes me back,' he breathed, then lifted his head. Beth looked up to question him. His expression was ambiguous. He took two slow steps towards his wing of the palazzo—stopped—and then turned, drawing her in the opposite direction instead.

'I thought perhaps you were going to sweep me off to your rooms, Luca.' She smiled, but her voice was hesitant, questioning.

'No, not tonight.' He shook his head.

She reached up. He had left his tie somewhere, and the top three buttons of his shirt were undone. She slipped her hand inside. He caught her wrist.

'I like to have a private bolt-hole, especially after evenings like this one. The pressure is on me to perform, to put on a good show and provide everything my guests want. And you wouldn't believe how much that is, *tesoro*. Everybody needs a piece of me. I have all the friends in the world—as long as I keep behaving exactly as *they* want, and handing out the cash.'

'That's terrible!' Beth was shocked. Her alarm was magnified a hundredfold as he started to laugh.

'And *that's* irony, coming from you.' He pulled her roughly against him and kissed her again. 'You made it bearable for me tonight, Beth. Seeing you at that party, keeping everyone entertained, but without running to me every few seconds was a revelation.'

So he *had* noticed her! That must be why he had been on the spot so fast when the drinks were spilled. Beth glowed with the idea of Luca watching her secretly all evening—her guardian angel, just as he had been in the past. Her heart was bouncing. This was the closest they had been so far, but she dared not let her feelings show. Luca was such a private man. To say something like that must have cost him a lot, and so she couldn't risk losing the ground she had gained. Mouth dry, heart pounding, she forced herself to keep her response low-key.

'I've learned to stand on my own two feet,' she said evenly as they reached the door to the bridal suite.

'And very beautiful feet they are.' He smiled.

Stopping, he gathered her into his arms for a long, lingering kiss. It swept every thought out of Beth's head as her body liquefied beneath his strong, warm hands. To feel him so close, wanting her after all the agony of separation… She knew with a certainty that burned like fire they must never be parted again.

'Oh, Luca…' she sighed as he eventually released her from paradise. Her hands slid from his soft dark hair to the flawless white of his shirt. In the darkness she heard his hand operate the door handle behind her. The door to her suite swung open and the rich warm fragrance of roses and lavender stole out to perfume the air around them. 'How I wish I'd never told you I was only going to work here for six months. Can I take it back? I'd do anything to keep this job at FFA. If only you knew…' She sighed, wishing she could tell him the whole truth about her love and her longing for him. But that was exactly what he *didn't* want to hear. Painful experience had taught her that, so she was careful to conceal her real meaning. 'I need *this job* so badly—'

His reaction was totally unexpected. Straight away, his hands began sliding down her body. They were ebbing away from her, his touch filled with regret.

'Of course you do. I suppose it's because of the money.' His voice became flat and cynical. 'How much do you want?'

'Nothing! Oh, Luca, I'd never ask you for money!'

'Why not? I get begging letters all the time. Why should you be different from anyone else?'

She stood back from him, alarmed. 'I don't want your money! I want *my* independence. That's never going to come through someone else's bank account, and certainly not yours.'

Although his hands abandoned her, his expression melted slowly from suspicion to curiosity.

'So what are you talking about?'

Beth drew in a long breath. It was painful. Luca had put the shutters up. He was standing before her, one hand in his pocket. The rattle of his loose change fell through the night like hailstones.

'When Dad died, he left enormous debts. I've had to sell virtually everything, Luca. The only thing left is a storage unit full of antiques. I was too sentimental to get rid of the things Dad loved when he died, but the time is coming when I'll have to do it.'

His face was grave. When he sighed now it was a faintly

irritable sound, not the low, smooth seduction that had filled her heart only a few moments earlier.

'I'm at my wits' end, but don't worry—I'm not expecting you to put in an offer, Luca. Dad may have spent a small fortune on antiques in total, but he was a magpie rather than a connoisseur. Even with my limited knowledge of the trade I know none of it will be of any interest to Francesco Fine Arts.'

There was enough light from a nearby table lamp to see he looked relieved at that, so she carried on.

'But I was wondering—I *do* need some information, Luca. It would only be to help me get the best prices. Although…after the way you spoke about Giulio Rosso's plans to make money out of his connections with FFA, I thought it best to be completely honest with you about it, as soon as possible.' She finished slowly, watching his expression for any signs of anger.

He caught the fabric of her skirt and pulled it through his fingers. The hissing sound it made rustled through the darkness between them.

'You are only passing through. Rosso may try to poach our business, which is why I resent his plans. It is not as though you would be setting up in opposition to me,' he said thoughtfully.

Beth breathed again. 'That's true. I'd be working in a completely different market, and hundreds of miles away—'

'So you really won't be staying in Venice?' he said quickly, but covered his reaction with a laugh. 'Oh, of course not—it will be cheaper to sell off Gerald's stock in England, to English people.'

'That's exactly what I thought.'

Beth started to think there might still be some hope for them, after all. She reached out her hand to him, but he appeared not to notice.

She tried harder. 'If you taught me the secrets of your success, Luca, I might be able to carry it further and actually set up in business on my own account.'

'Of course.' His voice was emotionless. 'As I said, it always comes down to money in the end.'

'I want a proper career, so no man thinks I'm going to sponge off him,' she said with steely determination.

'Andria won't thank you for thinking PA work isn't a proper career.'

'I didn't say that, because it is,' Beth said, keen to defend her choices. 'I love the job I'm doing now, but I'm never going to progress while I'm working for Ben. It's like re-inventing the wheel every day. I need more satisfaction from my life, Luca. And I intend to find it,' she finished meaningfully.

He did not act on the hint that she had changed. A sudden shaft of moonlight lit his face. But his expression no longer held the promise of seduction she so desperately needed. The light in his eyes was guarded now, not teasing.

'All right, Beth. I'll see what I can do. A masked ball, followed by a little nepotism and intrigue—what could be more fitting in a place like this?' He raised his arm towards the vaulted ceiling in a furl of silk.

'Luca! I'm being serious.' She laughed, and tried to cuff him playfully. For a second it was the old days all over again as he caught her raised hand.

'So am I.'

Then he bent his head close to hers, and his lips brushed her on the forehead.

This time it was nothing more than a kiss between friends, Beth thought with a falling heart. She had spoiled it all again. Luca was showing her business and pleasure did not mix. Why hadn't she realised he would think like that? He was a professional, above all things. Mentioning her plans had driven a wedge between them, when she had been so desperate to avoid it.

'I don't want to rely on anyone else ever again, Luca,' Beth said when she had swallowed her disappointment.

'Good. That's very good—and exactly what I would want.' He nodded. 'So I'll think about it…'

His voice whispered like a dream as his hands rested on her neck. Then his touch moved lightly over her shoulders. The rasp of his fingers against her satin skin made her tingle with anticipation.

But then he withdrew his touch and turned to walk away. Before Beth could swallow her disappointment, he threw some words over his shoulder.

'There—I've thought about it, Beth. I'm flying to Paris tomorrow. Come with me.'

She was staggered.

'Luca…what are you saying?'

He turned back to look at her. 'I need a top-class PA on hand for my meetings next week. What I don't need is a girl who can't survive without a man. I normally spend any downtime doing research, networking and making new contacts. You can watch, and learn as I do it. It will be your introduction to working my way, in this business. You'll have a week to show me how willing you are.'

'And what will you want in return, Luca?' she asked, hardly daring to hope.

He laughed.

'From you, Beth? Not a cent. All I'm offering is a temporary position as my PA. You've managed to work for Ben Simpson for this long without murdering him. That proves to me you are the world's best at the job—hard-working, an independent thinker, discreet and loyal. This trip to Paris will show if you've got the spirit to translate those skills into a different arena. You'll exchange your qualities for my expertise and contacts.'

Just when she thought she had lost him again, Luca was offering her the chance to work at his right hand. She would be spending every minute of her working day beside him. The whole idea made Beth feel light-headed, but one tiny corner of her mind carried on working.

'What about Andria? You can't just replace her with me!'

'That's not a problem. Andria knows better than to challenge any decision I make. But if you were wondering about the effects this trip might have on your friendship with her…how badly do you want to make this career change?'

Beth swallowed hard. 'I've only ever wanted one thing more, Luca.'

He gave a slow, satisfied smile. 'That's not on offer, I'm afraid.'

Startled at his tone, Beth opened her eyes wide. Her reaction amused him.

'You will have to make do with just my company, Beth.

My fortune and my palazzo are most definitely off *this* menu.'

'Why should I think otherwise? What do you mean?' She gasped, following him towards the stairs.

'Don't look like that. It's perfectly obvious what I mean. While we are in Paris I shall be offering you the benefit of my knowledge and experience, while you work as my PA. And then as evening falls...' he paused, and then made a totally impulsive gesture: reaching out, he pushed his fingers through the fine luxuriance of her soft blonde hair again and cradled her head in his strong, square hand '...we will each return to our own private suites.'

Her heart stood still. How could he talk like that, but touch her like this, with such tenderness? Beth knew she would never be able to resist him, but Luca's self-control was legendary. Or at least it had been, once upon a time...

Two could play the temptation game. However much it hurt, Beth decided she had to pretend to turn off her feelings to order, in the same way he did.

'All right.' She nodded, stepping away from his touch. 'When do we leave for Paris?'

Her voice was husky with anticipation, but Luca stilled it with a sentence.

'Early in the morning, which is why I must leave you right now,' he murmured, reaching out to give her cheek a final, idle caress. Turning away, he started along the landing. His final words were thrown casually over his shoulder.

'And thanks again for being such a great success at the party this evening, *cara*. I'm glad you enjoyed it!'

She stared after him, lost for words. He kept giving her the sweetest possible hints of what she had been missing for so long. How could he walk away every time, leaving her body simmering with this boiling need for him?

Luca strolled toward his room, wondering why he didn't feel good about what had just happened. He'd proved once again Beth had no hold over him. However powerful his physical need for her, he could still master it.

Then his expression altered. Beth had surprised him. In Balacha, she had told him it was marriage or nothing. Tonight, she had come up with the idea of forging herself a career. Perhaps she had changed…but then, look at the way she had jumped at the chance to visit Paris with him. They might be going as boss and PA, but they would be staying in the most romantic city in the world…

A sudden riot of pain in his lower back made him stop with a gasp. Before Beth Woodbury had walked back into his life, he would have blamed it on too much dancing. Now it was memories of one fateful night in Balacha twisting the knife. Black thoughts crowded in on him again.

What if she hadn't totally given up the idea of ensnaring him? This might be the chance she was looking for, to seduce him.

He checked his watch and then took a few slow steps, testing himself. The pain eased, but never really went away. When it returned like this, it brought back all those agonising memories.

As he paused in the silence the cold moon showed its

face again. Shafts of silvery light streamed into the gallery. It skimmed the nearest statue, striking bitter sparks from Apollo's marble fingers as he tried to possess a nymph.

Luca looked at his own hands. Only moments before, they had been pressed against Beth's skin. It did not take much to imagine her warm softness under his fingertips now. He looked at the tormented marble figures beside him. The sculptor had frozen their frustration for all time— a god doomed to lust after the one thing he could never have. In a few hours' time, Luca would be taking Beth to Paris, with no need to worry about any consequences. They had an agreement. He needed a PA. All she wanted—she said—was a career, and while she was working for him he could teach her. That was all there was to the bargain. Once trained, she would disappear from his life again as suddenly as she had entered it. And that would be the end of their story.

Luca began to feel strangely uneasy. He tried to shake off the sensation. It was impossible. He had no idea why his mind kept returning to the idea of Beth going away. After all, it wouldn't be the first time she had left him. He ought to be used to it. And back in Balacha, he would have been delighted if she'd started showing some independence. She hadn't managed to tie him down then, so if she wanted to strike out now he ought to be pleased. His life was his own, and if Beth got as much satisfaction out of her future career as he got from his…

He grimaced again, and dropped his hands to his side in irritation. Then he straightened up and force-marched on towards his suite. Whatever his body might be telling him, he refused to be trapped by anything: lust, pain or any

woman—especially Beth Woodbury. Right now, part of it
was becoming as rigid as the statue of Apollo, but Luca
knew he could conquer the feeling. When it came to Beth
he could take her, or he could leave her alone, he reassured
himself. If her interest in the fine-art business was more
than a whim, the trip to Paris could be a vital part of her
education. It meant nothing to him, other than the fact she
was there to act as his personal assistant.

By the time he reached his rooms, Luca had rational-
ised all his problems away. Dropping his masquerade mask
on a chair, he went straight into his bedroom. Pouring out
a long glass of iced water, he took a couple of painkillers.
He counted the minutes until they took effect, his fingers
dancing over the only good thing to come out of Balacha.
It lay on his bedside table. Silvia the housekeeper insisted
all his other medals should be on display in one of the
cabinets in the dining hall. Luca refused to have this one
stared at, and commented on by his guests. It stayed in his
private rooms, which were out of bounds to everyone
except Silvia. Everything else he valued was locked away,
out of sight.

The pain gripped him again. He put a clenched fist to
the small of his back, using pressure to counteract it. What
he needed was distraction. The contents of that secret compartment inside his dressing chest were guaranteed to
deflect his mind. Crossing the room, he opened the top
drawer and operated a hidden catch.

The compartment held only two things: a photograph,
and a seashell threaded onto a fine gold chain. The
necklace was broken, its delicate fastening torn wide open
and useless. Luca picked it up. For a while, he had carried

it with him everywhere. But, unlike pain, even Beth's fragrance had disappeared eventually. Now her broken necklace lived here, instead of in his wallet. Tonight, its chain swung between his fingers like a pendulum marking time. Turning the shell around to catch the light, he studied it intently. Delicate as sea-washed porcelain, it was iridescent with mother-of-pearl.

The pendant had kept all its colours, but the snapshot stored with it had not lasted so well. Cheap film and a throw-away camera meant it had faded badly. Luca placed the necklace carefully back onto its bed of cotton wool. Then he picked up the photograph and looked at it closely. Every detail was still there, although he didn't need to look at it to remind himself what they were. The photograph was of Beth, and she was smiling. Her expression spoke to him clearly now, but at the time he had been too busy to listen. The picture showed a girl who had completely convinced herself she was in love. As the shutter clicked she had expected him to feel the same way—as if it were her God-given right to be adored.

Luca went over all the old arguments. Her talk of marriage had been the final touch-paper. From birth, other people's expectations had mapped out his life for him. He had been packed off to board at the best schools. Later he had become a soldier, always with the unspoken understanding he would bring honour to the Francesco family name in everything he did.

But now Luca was the only one left. He was in total control, and calling all the shots. He had more money than anyone could ever spend, and he could do what he liked.

Everything about his life had changed completely over the past five years.

Everything, except the perfect seashell Beth had once worn around her neck.

CHAPTER SEVEN

BETH took her time getting undressed. Her mind was too full to think of sleep. Luca's passion ebbed and flowed like the sea, but she was continually at high tide. She wanted him so much—why did he always shut her out at the last moment? She stroked the heavy velvet of her gown with the same wistful longing she wanted to use on him. Packing all her masquerade clothes away with her dreams, she got into her lonely bed. For a long time sleep was impossible. Luca was only metres away, and the thought kept her mind racing. When at last she managed to doze, vivid dreams of him rolled her about fitfully until she woke up hot with expectation. Her mind and body were already alight with the thought of travelling to Paris with him. He was such a seasoned traveller he probably wasn't giving it a second thought, but Beth's mind was full of it.

She was ready to go down to breakfast long before it was light. By the time he walked in, she was idling over her second cappuccino. The moment he swung into view she stood up and created his first coffee of the day.

'One macciato, with a teaspoonful of Demerara sugar.'

'You remembered.'

He looked impressed, but then his face fell. 'Although I gave up sugar a long time ago.'

'This much won't kill you.'

He took a sip, and smiled.

Wanting to keep the approval in his eyes, Beth went over to the buffet table. It was loaded with enough fresh fruit, juices and bakery to feed an army. Everything was set out in crystal bowls or wicker baskets lined with mono-grammed liners. She picked up a neatly folded napkin, and a plate.

'Have what you like.'

'I've already finished mine. This is for you.' She began looking over the rolls, already wondering whether he would prefer a seeded roll, a pastry or crackers. Luca curled his lip.

'Thanks, Beth, but no.' He moved forward sharply, abandoning his coffee and taking the plate from her hands. 'This arrangement of ours will be strictly business.'

She looked up, slightly flushed with embarrassment. 'Fine—then I'll get on with programming my laptop.' She sat down and began fiddling with her computer.

'You've started work already?' He sounded impressed.

'Of course. Don't forget, I saw how you worked in—' she hesitated, changing what she had been about to say '—in the past. The way Andria's always kept so busy must mean nothing has changed.'

'That's true,' Luca said bitterly.

He passed behind her to take his place at the dining table. Watching him pull out his chair and sit down, Beth winced at the way his hand-crafted suit emphasised the lean lines of his body. Luca always looked smart, but he rarely looked satisfied.

Beth waited until he had settled himself before she began to speak. 'Now, *signor,* I need to feed your timetable into this thing…'

He reached into his pocket and slid his organiser across the table towards her. Without looking up, Beth began going through the entries.

'The first thing I must do is ring Andria and explain—'

'I've done it.' He dipped one end of a croissant into a pool of strawberry conserve, but paused when he saw Beth's look of concern.

'She's fine.' He smiled. 'I told her she could move in here, at the palazzo, for a week of luxurious living free of charge.'

With a sigh of relief, Beth went back to studying his timetable.

'You don't have anything scheduled for tomorrow morning….' She looked up, confused.

'It's because I've cancelled a working breakfast to make time for teaching you,' he said, chasing a last few crumbs around his bone china breakfast plate.

Beth stared at him in horror. 'Luca! I mean—Signor Francesco. You can't do that, just for me. I'll ring whoever it was, and explain there's been a mistake—'

'No, you won't.' Luca reached out. His hand went over hers, stopping her busy fingers. She looked up.

'*Petit dejeuner* with the Comte was going to be as much a social occasion as anything else, and you know how much I enjoy those.'

She smiled at him, but his attention was elsewhere.

Standing up, he went over to the buffet and brought back a whole basket of rolls and a glass dish of low-fat spread. After peeling an almost white flake off the block of margarine, he dropped the knife in disgust.

Beth had been trying not to notice, but that was too much for her to bear. Without a word, she fetched a replacement knife from the buffet—along with a crystal bowl of sunflower-yellow butter.

'You can blame me for leading you astray, *signor*.'

'Thank you.'

She pretended to study his organiser, but watched him all the time from beneath her lowered lashes. He spread the butter over the soft white bread of his roll with great care. When he took a bite it was with real relish. Hiding a smile, Beth tapped the stylus on the screen of his organiser to concentrate her mind on the job in hand.

'Right—I've finished transferring everything, so it looks as though my last question for the moment is…what time would you like your alarm call set in the morning, *signor?*'

'Ten minutes before yours.'

Luca's voice was low with meaning. Beth looked up to find his dark eyes twinkling at her over the rim of his coffee-cup. 'I shall call it my independence time. The only moments I'll be able to call my own.'

'All right, I can take a hint!' She laughed, and began to pack her things away. 'I'll leave you to enjoy the rest of your breakfast; although there's one more thing I need to ask. Can I go and pick up a few books from the palazzo library to read on our flight?'

'There's a selection all ready for you, piled up on the table nearest the window.'

'Thank you, that's great.' Beth was relieved, and it gave her enough confidence to ask a second question. 'I've transferred all those mysterious little symbols peppered through your schedule into my own diary, but where can I find out what they mean?'

'You can't.' He concentrated on buttering another roll. 'They don't mean anything to anyone but me.'

'But as your PA—'

'Beth, you don't need to know. Trust me.'

'Fine. OK.'

Beth carried on getting ready to leave the table. When she handed him his organiser, he moved forward slowly as though he could hardly believe she was doing it in silence.

'That's it? You mean you aren't going to argue?'

He was looking at her with curiosity. Turning away, Beth headed for the dining-room door.

'Nope.'

Her reply was offhand, and she didn't look at him. She couldn't. His reaction told her everything she wanted to know. It filled in the gaps between all the hints dropped by his party guests the night before. The code must mean Luca's appetite for women was as rampant as ever. There could be no other explanation.

It's just *me* he doesn't want, she thought, feeling her heart turn inside out.

With delight, Beth found Luca did not travel by scheduled airline. When they got to the airport, a private plane was waiting for them on the tarmac. She recognised its crest immediately. It was the same design used all around the palazzo, from its doors to the bed linen. A smartly dressed steward escorted her up the steps and into the plane. There, she was settled in a roomy armchair-like seat. She almost had to pinch herself as a second man handed her a tall glass of freshly squeezed orange juice. It was almost like going on holiday, and it had been years since Beth had been able to afford one of those. Now she was being waited on hand, foot and finger. It was incredible. Not only was she relaxing in a space that looked and felt like an executive lounge, she had a personal flight attendant. Among other things, he told her there was a fully equipped bathroom on board.

'You could almost live on this plane,' Beth joked as Luca joined her in the cabin.

'It's possible. The bedroom is behind us,' he replied, but kept his smile for the steward who greeted him with a run-down of travel conditions. 'Although it won't be needed today. You'll be glad it's a short flight for once, Sam,' he added as the steward handed him a drink.

There was always real warmth in Luca's tone when he talked to his staff. It never failed to catch at Beth's heart. She longed for him to speak to her like that, but he was already being handed his laptop. As he plugged into the on-board business facilities he spoke without looking up.

'Please excuse me, but I've got a mountain of work to deal with. If you need anything, Sam or the others are constantly on hand.'

He settled into one of the wide seats and logged onto his computer. The steward showed Beth how to access the power circuit herself, assuming she would be working, too. With a flutter of horror, she realised she had not thought of it.

'Oh, no! I didn't think there would be time to do anything, so everything is packed away in my case.'

'Fetch it for her, would you, please, Sam?' Luca said pleasantly, but the look he gave Beth was piercing. 'You can get a lot done in only half an hour, if you put your mind to it.'

'I know. That's why I'm going to start the moment I get my books.' Beth tried to sound professional, but she was kicking herself for making such an error.

His answering smile made sure she wouldn't make such a mistake again.

Beth kept her eyes on her books but her mind was always a couple of metres away, totally focussed on Luca. His presence meant everything to her. She was desperately conscious of the effect he was having on her body, even when he was busy with his work. Although he was miles away, lost in his correspondence, she was liquid with the nearness of him. They were surrounded by all this luxury, and with the temptation of a bedroom almost within reach—yet Luca had never felt further away.

As the plane taxied along the runway Beth felt her heart-beat increase. She tried to distract herself by looking out of the window. It did no good. Nothing could ever stop her wanting Luca. The one thing she desired so much her body ached with need was the single thing he held in his power to deny her, now and for ever.

The jet lifted off, but her heart remained painfully grounded.

A glossy limousine was waiting for them at the airport. Beth expected it to be a hire car, so when Luca greeted the chauffeur by name she was astonished.

'Is this man employed by FFA too?' she asked as they were swept towards the city.

'He works for me, yes.' Luca leaned back with the slightly bored air of a regular traveller. 'I own the apartment in Paris, and as I lead such a busy life it's easier to keep it permanently staffed. I often pop over here for a few days, and it means I can walk in and out without putting Andria to the trouble of making fresh hotel arrangements each time.'

'Are you staying there now?'

'We both are.'

His eyes flickered. There was a pause, and then he looked away from her and out of the window. It had been a tiny, involuntary gesture but Beth's heart had flipped at exactly the same moment. Just the mention of sleeping arrangements fired a starting pistol in her head. Now all her senses were racing with the thought of sharing his apartment. Had Luca's eyes betrayed the same feelings? Beth spent the rest of their journey wondering. Staying in Paris with Luca would be part dream, part nightmare. He was tantalisingly close, but every time she tried to make a move he shut her out. While he kept raising this invisible barrier between them, he could never be near enough for her.

When they reached the city, their limousine came to a halt in an exclusive *arrondisement*. Beth assumed it was something to do with traffic restrictions. When the chauffeur got out and opened the car door for her, it took a few seconds to realise they had arrived. Luca's apartment was in one of the most beautiful avenues in the world—and one of the most expensive. When he joined her for the short walk across its wide pavement, he looked almost pleased.

He ought to be, she thought as a uniformed commission-aire appeared at the doors of a tall, gracious building. Luca greeted him like a friend, and introduced Beth. The man looked momentarily surprised, but managed to hide it from his employer. Only Beth noticed, and it made her feel uneasy.

The marble entrance hall was tiled like a Roman villa, inlaid with mother-of-pearl and decorated with classical scenes. It didn't feel like Luca's style at all. Not that I know what that is any more, Beth thought. He's a different man from the one I loved in Balacha. But then, the feelings she had were different, too. Her need for him had never changed, but now she was in awe of his success, and pleased at the way he had achieved it through his own hard work.

'The apartment is divided in two—one half for working, the other for living.' Luca explained as they headed towards the lift. 'You can get to the offices from this lobby. And there's a connecting door from my personal suite, too.'

There was that look in his eyes again—wary, and fleeting. He had been careful to turn away as he spoke, but Beth still saw it—or thought she did. She brushed a hand across her forehead, in case she was running a temperature. Her skin was cool to the touch. Her feelings were red-hot, but Luca remained as collected as ever. He ushered her into a glass-sided elevator and they were whisked up to a land of polished parquet floors and lush potted palms. Luca's living rooms were airy, spacious and the last word in gracious living, but they lacked any personal touches. There were some exquisite pieces of antique furniture, and a small rainforest of greenery. But there were no photo-graphs on the grand piano, or ornaments on the high marble mantelpieces. Floral arrangements burst like fireworks from the cold hearths and glass-topped tables. They made the room look beautiful, without feeling loved. Beth strolled over to the windows. Luca reached them first. Opening the French doors, he led her out onto a balcony.

'Isn't this view over the Avenue Foch wonderful?' He gestured across at façades almost as grand as his own building.

'You won't be able to see it for much longer.' Beth nodded towards the filigree of climbing roses trained up from big lead planters hemming the balcony. A few late lemon flowers billowed over the carefully colour co-ordinated petunias around their feet.

'I need the countryside, and this is the nearest I can get to it.' He pointed out over the iron railings. A wide expanse of grass separated them from the road. It was planted with street trees, but they were already losing their leaves. Stark skeletons would soon be all that stood between Luca and the city.

'And I've never felt further away from Rose Cottage.' Beth sighed.

'This isn't a place to feel gloomy.'

Luca's rich Italian accent made his words sound almost caressing, but his expression was still guarded. 'We'll start work on your studies straight away. Then you won't have time to be homesick, and you will be closer to starting your new career. The sooner that happens, the sooner you can pay off your debts and settle back in your very own house. That's what you want, isn't it?'

He managed a smile, and Beth wondered if she would ever be able to think of her decaying old home and do the same.

* * *

Luca worked her hard, but Beth was a willing slave. It was worth taking pages of notes, just for the pleasure of being with him. And it was not all work. His staff at the apartment packed them snacks of quails' eggs, cheeses and fruit to keep up their strength between coffee breaks. When Luca wasn't entertaining clients or being entertained, they jumped on and off almost every stop on the metro, visiting dozens of places, walking for miles, and idling over every salon in the Louvre. There, to her delight, Luca showed her the secret lives of paintings. In discovering why pictures looked as they did, she learned to stop hating everything she didn't understand.

'Always remember: not everyone shares *your* idea of what is beautiful,' he told her. 'When you are buying on behalf of clients, they look for value for money. Ask yourself if their investment is likely to increase.'

'But I thought the first rule of buying art was to spend only what you could afford to lose?'

'That's gambling—something we never do at Francesco Fine Arts.' Luca's absolute honesty showed in his face. 'Our clients are ready to spend vast amounts, in order to diversify their investment portfolios. FFA must find treasures worthy of them. It's a tricky job, but satisfying when everything goes right. For example, last year I picked up a piece by a rising star for an internationally famous actor. Within months, publicity for the painter's other work caused it to almost double in value.'

'Who were you buying for?' Beth looked into his face, desperate for clues. His smile gave nothing away.

'That's another important lesson for you, Beth. Absolute discretion is the way to gain a client's trust, and their future business. Especially if they are a regular at the Oscars.' He strolled over to a bench and sat down.

'I used to be the first one who wanted to find a seat,' Beth said as she followed him. Luca did not seem to have heard her.

'It's been a long day, Beth. You must have writer's cramp from taking all those notes. I think we'll head back to the apartment.'

They were on their way home along one of the grand boulevards when they passed a shop with hardly anything in the window. Beth knew the less there was on display, the more exclusive it was. She stopped. Luca strolled on a few paces before he realised she was no longer at his side.

'What's the matter?' he frowned.

'Come and look at this beautiful rug! Its design has all the tension and colour of Miro, but with the soft luxuriance of chenille. The contrast of modern style and retro fabric is amazing.'

Luca laughed. 'You're a quick study, aren't you? No wonder you've made such a success of being Ben's PA in so short a time.'

It was the first time Beth had seen him look really happy. She smiled, and for a fraction of a second they had something to share. But, elusive as a falling leaf, it was gone with the next breath. They looked away from each other, and Beth blushed in confusion. Everything felt so right— but only for an instant. Now they were two strangers looking in a shop window again.

From the corner of her eye, Beth saw Luca make a sudden movement. Without meaning to, she glanced at him. He was grimacing as though a sudden pain had gripped him. Realising she was looking, he focused his expression to impassive and slipped one hand inside his jacket.

'It isn't fine art, but if you really like it, Beth, I'm sure my accountants won't mind.'

Pulling out his wallet, he headed into the shop. Beth chased after him.

'You'd buy it for me?' she gasped as he passed one of his credit cards to the watchful shop assistant.

'Why not?' He sounded surprised. 'You've been working well, Beth. Call it encouragement, to keep you working just as hard in the future.'

'Are you sure?' she said as the assistant hesitated, looking from one to the other and back again. 'I mean, I know you were pleased with the way I handled your party, but you don't have to be quite so generous.'

'Why not?' Luca gazed at her as though he could hardly believe anyone would try and stop him spending money. 'If money was no object to you, you'd buy it for yourself in a flash.'

'I'd trample over any other customer to get it.' Beth looked back at the window display, ravishing it with her eyes. 'But you can't buy me something like this! I'm only your PA.'

'That's true—but I've been watching the way you work.' There was no flirtation in Luca's expression, only his trademark honesty. Beth could hardly believe it. In the past their relationship had been one of extremes. He'd seduced her, he'd been angry with her, but he had never spoken to her like this before. It was as though he might be starting to believe in her ability to do something more than simply give and receive pleasure. 'So if you want it, Beth, then it's yours. I'd do exactly the same for Andria.'

She looked into his eyes, and saw it was true. Her heart sank. For a few precious seconds she had almost believed this might be a sign her romance with Luca could be re-kindled. Now she saw his gesture for what it was—a present for a good employee.

While she was distracted, he let go of his plastic.

'And I can think of it as an investment too, Beth. You'll need something to furnish your prestige office, when you start your new career.'

The moment the assistant saw the name on his client's card, he spoke into a discreet microphone beside the till. While Beth was still trying to work out if Luca's latest comment was a compliment, the shop's owner material-ised. He smiled and bowed to them from behind the counter.

'Signor Francesco! I was not aware you were due to visit us today?' he said in a well-bred whisper. 'If I had known, rest assured you would have been met at the door, as usual—'

'Don't worry, Pierre. We were just passing. This is an impulse buy.' Luca smiled. The owner and his assistant relaxed instantly. Beth marvelled again at Luca's knack of putting people at their ease, until he began to talk about delivery details.

He turned to look at Beth. 'You can't have it sent to Rose Cottage if you aren't going to be there for months. Although...' he tapped his fingers on the edge of the counter '...it might be better to have it sent straight to your rooms in the palazzo. Put a note with the delivery that it must be sent direct to the bridal suite at my Venice address, would you, Pierre?'

'Ah—so congratulations are in order, Signor Francesco.' The shop owner and his assistant smiled still more.

He laughed, dismissing their congratulations. 'No—my colleague Beth is learning the business. I'm writing the cheques at the moment, as it'll be a while before she can do it herself,' Luca said smoothly. 'And don't bother logging this on the business account, Pierre. It's a personal transaction.'

Beth went red-hot from top to toe. It was beginning to sound as though Luca really did believe she might make it one day. It was a lot to live up to, and it made her think.

'You've gone very quiet,' he said a while later as they waited on the platform of the metro.

'My mind is spinning like a mouse on a wheel,' she said, when she could find the words.

'I can guess. As I said in the shop, you've been working hard today.'

He put his hand to her elbow. Beth looked up, and thought she saw a glow of real pride in his eyes. Then their train arrived, and he moved her to the edge of the platform. He was careful to make sure the doors did not close before she was safely on board. There was only one empty seat, which he gestured for her to take, standing himself. She felt as if he were protecting her, when really she knew he was only being a gentleman.

'You must let me pay you back for the rug as soon as I can.' She tried to recapture the moment as they were reunited on the Avenue Foch. He shook his head in a good-natured way.

'You were such a fast learner when it came to style and substance, it was a pleasure to buy you something as a reward.'

'And you don't expect anything in return, Luca?' she said slowly.

He did not look at her, so this time his eyes remained a mystery. But his voice was firm.

'We have an agreement this trip is about work, and nothing else. You know you can always trust me, Beth.'

'Of course I do. You're the most honourable person I know.'

With no answer, he turned right away from her and pulled back the sleeve of his jacket. But instead of checking the time, he swore softly.

'What's the matter, Luca?'

'I've lost my watch.'

He stopped and looked back along the wide avenue. 'I had it when we left Pierre's shop...'

Beth paused, recounting the last few minutes in her head. 'Don't worry. It can only have gone in the last hundred metres or so. I asked you the time before we agreed to stop at that magazine stand, remember?'

They started back along the pavement, scanning every centimetre. Beth had reached the knot of people jostling around the newsagent before turning to Luca, admitting defeat. 'Sorry, but I can't see it anywhere.'

'Neither can I. There's such a crowd here. I was distracted, so the strap might have broken at any time. It may even have been stolen,' he finished grimly.

Beth shook her head. 'That would be an awful thing to have happened! I'll contact the police for you. There are plenty of honest people around, though, so if it fell off innocently, it might have been handed in. Let me have a description, and I'll get onto it straight away.'

'You know what my watch was like. Although you're hardly in a position to buy me another one now.' He almost smiled.

'You mean it really *is* the same one I gave you, so long ago?' Beth stared at him. 'You're still wearing it?'

'It was a good watch. There's no point in abandoning something that worked so well.'

'No,' Beth said thoughtfully.

CHAPTER EIGHT

LUCA was silent all the way back to the apartment. Beth was worried. She had a plan in mind. It seemed to have got off to a good start, but now she was beginning to have second thoughts.

'I'm really sorry about your watch, Luca.'

'It doesn't matter.'

She relaxed, at least for a moment. Luca could have afforded every watch in any jeweller's showroom they passed, yet he hadn't considered stopping to buy a new one. Could she dare to hope that it held more than just monetary value for him?

She looked up at him and said, 'All the diaries are flagged up with reminders, and cross-referenced. You can leave everything to me, Luca. It's my job to make sure you never miss anything.'

'I miss my watch,' he joked sardonically.

They walked on in silence. She noticed he still kept moving his right hand toward his left sleeve, but each time he remembered a little bit sooner. She might have smiled, but something else concerned her.

'Are you sure there's nothing else wrong, besides your

watch?' she said eventually. 'You look as though you've got a lot of things on your mind, Luca.'

'I'm fine,' he said, but did not look at her.

When they reached his building, he went straight towards the door leading to his office complex.

'You can finish work now, Beth, but I must check my e-mails and log into the FFA computer system. Business doesn't stop just because I'm not there to deal with it in person. But, of course, you'll want to go out after dinner—to take in a show, or something.'

He glanced at her then, and managed a half-smile. Beth almost laughed with relief. She was keen to ease all the tension that was so visible in his face. Some time off together might help.

'Marie is the name of the girl in charge of the social side here. Let her know what you would like to do, and she'll arrange it for you—'

Beth sighed. Once again he had considered her—but not in the way she desired. 'No, thank you, Luca.'

It was all too obvious he expected her to go out on her own. He didn't intend taking her anywhere himself.

Disappointed but unable to give up, Beth tried again. 'I really don't fancy going out a second time today, Luca. I'd much prefer a quiet evening here.' *Together,* she added silently.

He gave her a penetrating stare.

'Now it's my turn to ask if *you* are all right, Beth?'

'I'm just a bit tired, that's all. It's been a hectic few days for me, rounded off with this route-march around the wonders of Paris. What I'd like more than anything else

would be to stretch out and relax in my room for a while.'
With you beside me, her body begged. She ached to invite
him, but could not bear to risk her feelings being trampled.
He had refused her often enough over the past few days.
She couldn't bear to be rejected again. It would spoil everything. At least if she kept her dreams to herself, she
could hang onto them for a little while longer.

Beth went straight to her room. She was so tired and disappointed she could no longer enjoy the cool, impersonal
beauty of her suite. She wandered from its cream drawing
room to the marble and silver wet room in a daze. Stripping
off her clothes as though they were as heavy as her heart,
she switched on the shower. She expected it to wake her
up, but it had the opposite effect. Later as she towelled her
hair dry her eyes began drooping. Switching on the sound
system, she selected some Mozart and settled at her desk
with a workbook of nineteenth-century designs. It was all
very interesting, but the sunshine was so low and bright it
made her squint, and while her eyes were half shut they
decided to go the whole way and then—and then—

Her elbow slipped off the desk, bouncing her awake.
This was ridiculous! She rang to ask housekeeping for a
double espresso in the hope of waking herself up. It might
have worked, if she hadn't decided to move out of the
direct line of the late sun streaming through the windows.
She went over to sit on her enormous feather bed to drink
it. The deep, downy softness of it was so comfortable and
relaxing after racing through the streets all day that not
even coffee could keep her from sliding gently into sleep…

* * *

Luca phoned down their order for dinner, but his mind wasn't on the job. He even forgot his own rule about only eating food in season. Thoughts of Beth were filling his mind so completely his chef had to ask him if he *really* wanted fresh asparagus in autumn.

The way she looked at him today was so different from the feral mischief he had known in Balacha. All the fun had evaporated from her. She'd become so serious. Those big blue eyes were trusting now, rather than wicked. And the way her small, neat hand flew across the paper as she noted everything he had told her was amazing. He never imagined she could work so hard. It was as though she really meant it, when she said she wanted a real career. She was trusting him to teach her everything. After seeing the way she worked, he was beginning to wonder if it would be enough. It wouldn't be long before she would have to move on, in search of paper qualifications. That would take money she didn't have at the moment. Luca guessed she wouldn't accept it from him, unless he put the case properly. She had tried to stop him buying that rug, after all, and the thing had cost less than a thousand Euros.

His conscience had been uneasy for a while, but today it was unbearable. There was only one thing to be done. He would go to her room now and explain that his impulsive offer to teach her might not be the best way for her to learn. She deserved a formal education. That needed money, and he was the man to provide it.

What's the worst that can happen if I offer to help? he thought, but still hesitated. Beth was a proud woman. She would probably grab her things and storm out.

Luca considered the consequences of that—he'd be

losing touch with her again, after she had started to show such promise...

Another sudden spasm in his back reminded him of Balacha. So what if she *does* walk out on me? Easy come, easy go, he told himself. And this time I'll be in the comfort of my own apartment, rather than under fire in some God-forsaken corner of a foreign airfield. I've said goodbye to her once, and if it happens again...well...

He took his time getting to Beth's suite. He half hoped to find her engrossed in one of her new glossy magazines, rather than working on one of the tasks he had set her. That would make her feel guilty, which would take some of the pressure off him. They would both be starting at a disadvantage.

Tapping on the door, he thought he heard a welcoming call. Opening it, he went inside and realised his mistake straight away. Beth's lounge was deserted, but the CD was playing. Still expecting to catch her shirking rather than studying, Luca moved silently to the open door of her bedroom. He was ready with a quick remark about slacking, but forgot it the instant he looked into her room.

Beth was curled on her side, fast asleep. Luca stopped. When he saw what she had been doing, he could not resist moving closer. He was enchanted. Her head was pillowed on one of the books he had given her. Far from wasting time as he imagined, she must have dropped off while working. Luca watched, hardly daring to breathe in case it disturbed her. The curtains fluttered in a breeze and her skin rippled with the chill it brought. Silently, he fetched a blanket from the nearest *armoire*. After laying it lightly over her, he eased the textbook from beneath her head, a millimetre at a time. He thought he had got away with it, but at the last moment Beth stirred and whispered his name with such feeling he stopped and caught his breath.

There was no way on earth he could resist her now.

It was a wonderful, unforgettable, heart-stopping mirage of a dream. Luca came to her through the darkness, bringing that well-loved feeling of warmth rushing through her body once more. She felt the familiar urge low in her belly as her muscles tensed with excitement. He rolled her over in the bed, holding her so tightly she plunged straight over the waterfall of orgasm. Helpless, all she could do was gasp his name, over and over again…

She opened her eyes. The dream vanished, but Luca was still there. He was fully clothed and standing beside her bed rather than naked and lying in it, but he was as gorgeous as ever.

'Luca! What are you doing here?' she squeaked, pink with confusion. Snatching up handfuls of bedclothes for cover, Beth threw herself over to the far side of the bed. Fantasy Luca was one thing—but to wake up with him bending over her… For an instant, dreams and reality mingled and she didn't know which to believe. It was as though she could still feel the caress of his lips on her cheek.

She touched the place Luca had kissed in her dream. It was burning like fire.

'I had to move this…'

Luca gestured to the workbook he had rescued and placed it on the table beside her. When he looked up she was caught in his gaze. He was poised, and she knew he was waiting for her. No language in the world could possibly convey the need and desire of that moment. Their minds and fantasies met and melded in silence. Too many words had passed between them already.

She shivered, and it broke the spell. Silently he turned away and went over to close the window. As she watched him Beth caught sight of herself in a mirror. What she saw there made her gasp. Her eyes were as large and dark as his, and there was a dewy glow on her skin. That only came from the sort of sex she had been dreaming about. For another wonderful, terrible moment she wondered if Luca *had* managed to ravish her as she slept. The idea made her smile. It was unthinkable. No woman could sleep while Luca was around! From behind her bundle of bedcovers, she became acutely aware of the warm perfume rising from her body. Beth's dream had seduced her into expecting a real-life encounter. When Luca padded back, she was ready. She dropped her defence and accepted him into her arms. His body enfolded her. They fitted together perfectly, as always.

'Let me warm you, *carissima.*'

His pupils were huge. A smile began playing around his lips, teasing her almost beyond endurance. As he held her against his body she could feel he was as physically aroused as she was.

She could hardly breathe with the excitement of it all. Her palms were damp, but she didn't care. She was in Luca's arms, and nothing else mattered. If only this moment could go on for ever… The suspense was wonderful and terrible at the same time. Would he walk away from her again? Would he stay? All the unspoken questions beaded her lashes.

His hands swept up to cup her head. And when he kissed her all her doubts and fears seemed a million miles away.

CHAPTER NINE

THEIR kiss was ten thousand times better than her wildest dreams. He overwhelmed her, and Beth was only too willing. Waking from her fantasy, she found that reality exceeded it. When Luca broke contact with her lips, he only stopped kissing her for long enough to murmur:

'Beth...*cara*...*tesoro*...how have I managed to resist you for so long?'

His voice had the husky depth of a testosterone rush. Beth knew she had to make a gesture for the sake of her self-esteem, but it could be nothing more than a token. The only barrier remaining between them was her fear of rejection. It was going to fall any second. Then her heart, soul and mind would be wide open for Luca to do exactly as he wanted.

'You took a risk, Luca,' she whispered, almost shyly. 'How did you know I wouldn't scream blue murder?'

He threaded her golden hair through his fingers, caressing her. 'You looked totally irresistible. How could you expect me to turn and walk away from such temptation, laid out before me? And we both know from experience exactly how good things can be between us. The need to be adored is so strong in you, it can't be hidden by anything else.'

The smoky quality of his accent thickened to the texture of wild *Maccia* honey: rich, sweet and full of the memory of summer.

Beth knew his touch came at a price, but she no longer cared. The same wisdom that made her desperate for him also warned she would be nothing more than his next conquest. Still she could not resist.

She would only be the latest in a long line. She had known that from the moment she'd seen him again. *He makes love to them all, but loves none of them. Getting into his bed will be no real triumph for me,* she thought bleakly. *It will be sex played as a game to his rules, as always.*

He moved against her, making no attempt to hide the ridge of his masculinity. Beth found it impossible to concentrate on anything else. With a superhuman effort, she managed to murmur something to remind them of the leap they were about to take.

'But you're the managing director of Francesco Fine Arts. I'm only your temporary PA. This must break every rule in the book—' she managed faintly.

Luca was unfazed. 'It's my company. I'm the one who makes the rules,' he said smoothly. 'I want you, Beth, right here and now. And I'm going to have you.'

Where she could think only of love, she new he focussed on sensations. And yet… She had been yearning for his touch constantly for five years. This would be a way of experiencing it, one last time. Here was a chance to recapture everything life could be, if only she could grab the moment.

But my heart will always want so much more…she thought. She tried to swallow and speak, but her mouth was dry.

Luca paused, but only until he realised Beth was in no state to reply. Then he continued, in a voice soft with seduction.

'This was bound to happen in the end, *carissima*. There is no need to fight it.'

He arched his eyebrows in silent invitation and, as always, was in no mood to wait. He plundered another incredible kiss, and her final defences crumbled. She was all his. Her smooth, curvaceous luxury was soft beneath his hands. He had craved this for so long, after sending her away from Balacha. No woman had come close to satisfying him since then. No woman could match Beth, either in temptation or performance. There could be none better.

He'd proved it to himself dozens of times, but until this moment she had been nothing but a painful memory to him. Now she was here in his arms again, he could put reality to the ultimate test. Surely she could never be as good in bed as he remembered? This one emotionless burst of lust was calculated to satisfy his body, while easing his mind. Their kiss after the party had proved he could still resist her if he wanted to, but right now he didn't want to. He was determined to have his way with her one last time. Then he could get on with his life.

He would cleanse himself of Beth Woodbury.

Beth's mind was in free fall. All her worries had vanished under the pressure of his first, mind-altering kiss. Now he was in complete control of her body. She was in heaven. His fingers ran over her skin, setting light to every nerve ending. She tingled with anticipation, willing him to fly her higher, to a place where pleasure became almost too much to bear. She pressed her naked body against his clothed one, revelling in the friction of his cotton shirt and leather belt against her skin.

'I thought you would never ask for this,' she breathed.

'You should know by now I take what I want. I don't need to ask.' He clamped one hand on her bottom while the other fastened on her shoulder. She was pinned to him like a butterfly, prized by a collector.

'Not that you're putting up much resistance,' he growled into her hair. 'Go on, fight me if you dare.'

His laughing challenge inspired her. Arching her back, Beth twisted in his grasp. He was not about to let her go, and they wrestled with a kiss full of the fierce joy of life. Lissom as a seal, she brought her body up, tempting him to lift her off the ground.

'No—onto the bed,' he ordered. Waiting until she settled provocatively on the spun silk of the duvet, he eased his body down next to hers. Then his kisses consumed her with fire, teasing her face and neck before encircling her breasts with a million stars of arousal. With a cry her head fell forward, her golden hair cascading and mingling with his raven waves as she curled her body around his and dug her fingers into the fine white fabric beneath his shirt. The cotton hissed as she dragged her nails across it in an ecstasy of delight.

'Please— Take it off,' she moaned, scrabbling to try and push her hands up beneath it. The crushing pressure of Luca's palms stopped her.

'I'm the one who decides when to do that,' his voice rumbled softly.

With one hand he grabbed the remote control for the curtains from her bedside table. A single keystroke sent the green velvet drapes swishing over the windows. Beth's room was transformed into a shadowy palace of secrets. Only a little sunlight filtered through, giving the room an air of underwater mystery. Dropping the remote, Luca began using both hands on her again. Gently appreciating her with the tips of his fingers, he stroked every inch as though her delicate skin held the promise of peaches. She revelled in his attention until the need to experience his body got the better of her. She reached for the buttons of his shirt but his hands dropped over hers, crushing them again.

'No. It's you who I want to be naked in this bed,' he murmured. His breath hissed with suppressed sexuality.

In seconds, her fingers loosened his belt. He was already hot and hard beneath her hands. When she worshipped him with the warm insistence of her mouth, he responded with a moan wrenched from the very core of his being.

His fingers traced the outline of her face, lingering over the soft pleasure of her lips. She moved, and caught his thumb between her teeth. Nibbling her way along the skin at the side of his hand, she reached the soft sprinkling of dark hair beginning at his wrist. It held the sweet fragrance of his body and she paused to inhale as Luca rolled on top of her. He knew how much she enjoyed the weight of him bearing down on her. With a fierce kiss of possession he compressed the hardness of his body against hers. She responded, pushing upwards to caress the most delicate parts of her body against him. Feeling her arousal grow, he dipped his head and took the peak of her nipple between his teeth, grazing it gently until she shuddered with anticipation. Her hands swept down to grip his hips. As she held him he rolled again, pulling her over on top of him so he could carry on caressing her bottom in the way she loved. Beth was hungry for his body. She wanted to savour it in every way. She swivelled her body around so she could pay more attention to his towering maleness. There was nothing Luca loved more than the sensation of her tongue playing over him, her kisses teasing him into a thrashing frenzy of arousal.

'Nobody does this as well as you…I was so wrong to think they could.' He sighed. Suddenly, everything was right between them, and always should have been. Beth felt the familiarity of his lust while he revelled in her willingness. The temperature rocketed, their bodies twining and dancing in white-hot desire. First she caressed him with her hair, twining its silken softness around him until he moaned with pleasure. When he could not stand it any more, he caught her shoulders and pulled her up the length of his body. She was as light as air, but the effect of his erection nuzzling against the soft warm folds of her femininity was too much for them both. With a surge of ecstasy their bodies united. Swept along in an eternity of desire, they rode the tidal wave of need together.

Luca exhaled and pushed his hand into the glory of her hair, twining it through his fingers. It was what he always used to do. Beth's smile faded. Those five painful years divided them. Their worlds had been spinning apart for all that time. She had lost her only chance to love, and he had spent the time discovering new pleasures with dozens of other women. She knew that much from office gossip. There had been no one else for Beth, and never would be. The last waves of pleasure lapping through her body were stilled by the knowledge this was the very last time she would experience such physical satisfaction. No man came within a million miles of Luca. If she could not have him, then she was doomed to live her life alone. She desperately wanted to put her arms around him now and hold him close for these last few moments together. It was impossible. He was sure to mistake the gesture. He would think she was trying to cling onto him. That would send him leaping out of her bed, and Beth wanted to treasure every possible second of his presence. It was so sad to think that keeping her hands off Luca at a time like this was the only way to keep him at her side. Any tiny gesture of affection might repel him.

Disappointment and desire escaped from Beth in one long sigh. 'It's such a shame to think we'll never experience any of this again, Luca.'

He stopped stroking her hair. Gradually, his hand rested a little more weight against the side of her head. And a little more… She held her breath. When he replied, his voice did not have its usual brisk edge.

'Beth, what we've just experienced was far too good to waste.'

Puzzled, she raised herself up on one elbow and looked into his face. He reacted with a wry smile.

'On this trip, Beth, I want you in my bed every night.'

Beth could hardly believe what she was hearing. He might not be giving her his heart, but just being close to him was something. 'You mean…we can do this again?'

'Of course.'

She could have kissed him, but did not dare. She made herself count to ten, slowly. Then she added another ten, desperate not to sound too keen. In Balacha she had made the mistake of giving him an ultimatum—marriage or nothing. Over the intervening years she had cross-examined herself a thousand times, trying to work out where it had all gone wrong. Eventually, she realised Luca was like a wild stallion. To tell him he must be roped and tied by marriage had been so wrong. If she'd used a different approach back then, they might never have parted.

As they lay together in today's soft shadows, she began to wonder. After all she had done, might there still be a chance for them? If she could manage to treat all this as casually as Luca, he might realise she had changed. He could become curious enough to care, despite the mess she had made of everything in the past. If Beth could convince him she didn't want to tie him down, he might realise commitment didn't need to be stifling. But it would mean keeping her desperate need for him under total control. Beth ached to nestle further into his touch, but she was so afraid he might take it the wrong way. Instead, she rolled off his body and backed against the warm security of him. He responded by encircling her with his arms. She smiled into her pillow, but did not move.

'You must be the second luckiest person in the world, after me,' she murmured to herself, and he laughed.

'How do you make that out?'

She twisted out of his arms and sat up, amazed. 'You have everything! A beautiful home in the centre of Paris, a palazzo, apartments, private jets and limousines—what else could anyone possibly want?'

'You'd be surprised.'

He eased himself onto his back and lay watching her as she found her discarded dressing gown, pulled it on and flicked her hair out from inside its collar.

'For instance—if you could have anything at all in the world, Beth, what would it be?'

She had to get off the bed. There was only one answer to that question, and it was too painful to think about while she was so close to him. All she wanted was his love, and he didn't have any to give her.

'Well…it would have to be a home of my own,' she said at last.

'You've got one—Rose Cottage.'

'No. I'm only a tenant there,' she said without thinking, and then bit her tongue. Telling him was a mistake, but she had gone too far to stop now. Luca was bound to probe, so she got in first with her explanation. 'The house belongs to my uncle. Since Dad died, I've been living there under sufferance. Although the family is far too polite to say it, they want me out so the old place can be sold.'

Beth frowned, annoyed with herself. She had meant to keep that from Luca, in case he thought she was asking for help.

She went over to the dressing table and picked up her brush. Running it through the thick waterfall of her blonde hair, she could see Luca reflected in the glass, over her shoulder. He looked concerned, rather than angry. It surprised her.

'I thought you'd be horrified if I told you, Luca, but it doesn't seem to bother you at all.'

'Do you want me to buy the house for you?'

'Certainly not!' Colour flared in her cheeks. She whirled around to confront him, but he was laughing.

'No, I don't believe you'd accept it from me as a gift!' He nodded. 'Don't say you're coming around to my way of thinking—that property has no meaning, other than as a place to live?'

Beth shook her head. 'You know I've never seen it like that. Houses are somewhere to put down roots, to settle and stay. That's why I'd really love to design my own home, so once I moved in I'd never have to leave again.'

When she said that, he frowned. She turned back to the dressing table, and heard a faint rasping sound as he ran his thumb backwards and forwards over his chin.

'I'd never thought of a house like that. But it brings me back to my point—I might have privilege, Beth, but I can no more live where I like than…your queen can, for example. I inherited the palazzo in Venice, and this apartment was bought to serve a practical purpose, not a whim. It's a rock-solid investment in the best part of town. The fact my clients are speechless when I invite them here is a bonus. Whether or not it's where I would choose to live never featured in my decision to buy it.'

Beth was curious now. 'So where *would* you like to live, if you had a completely free choice?'

He stretched lazily, a sable cat in a sliver of evening sunlight as it slid through a gap between the closed curtains.

'There is no point in considering a question like that. I

have no choice. I must live in the Palazzo Francesco, and that is all there is to it.' He pulled her pillow over to his side of the bed and propped himself up on it. 'But tell me about your dream home. You really would not want to buy Rose Cottage?'

'Yes, of course I would, but the real fantasy is to have so much money I could keep my old home and build a better one, with all the mistakes of centuries ironed out.'

'I like the idea.' He smiled. 'Rose Cottage certainly has its share of problems. So you will make sure your next house has plumbing that doesn't gurgle and bang all night, keeping your guests awake?'

'Most definitely. And it will be a totally mouse-proof zone, too.'

'But with plenty of room for your horses.'

Beth put down her hairbrush and went into the dressing room of her suite. Finding something to wear for dinner gave her a chance to hide her pain from Luca as she spoke.

'Sasha and Foxy have been sold. Before I got the job as Ben's PA, I had a lot of temporary positions. When I was away from home, I couldn't give them the attention they deserved. They love people so much, it seemed fairer to let them go to a place where they would get plenty of exercise and be spoiled rotten at the same time.'

'But you loved them.'

'Love isn't always enough. Sometimes it's better to let go and keep your distance,' Beth murmured.

She had learned to set everything free. Everything— except for the memory of Luca.

* * *

Each time Beth and Luca made love it was better than the last. She had thought their experiences in Balacha were unbeatable, but this outshone it. Luca was like an avalanche, overwhelming her at every turn. He took her body with an urgency unusual even for him. Beth was quite happy to let him set the pace. Nowhere was safe from him. The only thing taking precedence over his body was her studies. Beth soon learned to hide her art textbooks when she heard his footsteps. If Luca thought he was going to interrupt her work, he would go off and distract himself with business.

To Beth's delight, Luca announced their time in Paris would be extended. He arranged everything. Andria was to move into Ben's office while they were away. She could just about manage to keep him under control, while being kept in touch with Luca's diary at the same time. This put Beth's mind at rest, and she was grateful. In the intervals when Luca abandoned her for the city, she had discovered a real thirst for knowledge. It was no hardship to fill her few spare hours with visits to the contacts Luca made for her. She was learning a lot about the art business. But she was also learning a lot about herself. Her father had supported her for so long, and then there had been her dreams of becoming a career wife. All that was behind her now. Now she had plans for real independence. For the first time, she realised she could become a success in her own right. She could not wait to put all her lessons into practice.

It was just as well she kept herself busy. Every time she stopped thinking about work, her mind was drawn back to how quickly she would lose Luca again. He kept stressing this was a temporary arrangement. Beth nodded when he said it, even though the idea was unbearable for her. So each time tears of regret began to threaten, she pulled herself away from him and headed for her desk. There, she plunged back into her textbooks. Filling her mind helped to dull her pain.

CHAPTER TEN

IT WAS all Beth could ever need. Luca wanted her more than ever. Work always came first, but he made plenty of time for play. For the next few days she was in a whirl of physical and mental arousal. When he had satisfied her body, he went on to stimulate her mind. She was in heaven. She could spend every waking moment with him. Better still, her work as his PA was actually managing to change him—for the better.

'What time is it, Beth?'

'Twenty minutes later than it was when you last asked me.'

He stopped studying one of da Vinci's virgins and looked at her with a glint in his eye.

'At least you've cured me of needing a time check every thirty seconds.'

Beth walked over to a bench. Sitting down, she swung her bag onto her lap and took out a bottle of mineral water.

'Here you go. It's almost time to consult that mysterious code in your organiser again.'

Luca strolled over and sat beside her. Taking a small

container from his inside pocket, he tapped a couple of small white pills into the palm of his hand.

He accepted the drink she offered.

'Originally, I thought it was women. But now I know differently,' she said. Watching him grimace as he took the tablets, she frowned too. 'I wish you'd tell me what you take them for, Luca.'

'You don't need to know, *cara.*' He frowned, his expression guarded. He was soon smiling again. 'In any case— what sort of a PA are you, if you haven't noticed I'm not taking so many pills now, or so often?' he teased.

'A polite and discreet one,' Beth countered, tucking the bottle of water back into her bag. 'Except when you're about to make yourself late for your next appointment!'

Luca could be as discreet as Beth, but everyone must have known about their affair. No lift needed to stop between floors *that* often, but none of the staff ever made any comment.

'You're sad to leave?' Luca noticed as he settled beside her in the Mercedes for their return trip to the airport. He loved driving, and often dismissed his chauffeur for the chance to get behind the wheel himself.

'Paris is a wonderful city. It's been so long since I had any sort of holiday, and working through it from the Louvre to the flea markets made me see the place in a completely different way. Not to mention all the bursts of excitement in between…' They shared a smile, but Luca was quick to become serious again.

'Yes, but there's something else. I can see it in your face, Beth.' He leaned in towards her, sliding his hand down her arm to take her hand. 'You are too pale. Is it because you didn't get much sleep last night?'

Beth smiled and shook her head. It was true she felt tired, but nothing would have made her admit it to him. She knew from now on she *had* to keep pace with Luca. The threat of being replaced in his life by the next willing woman tortured her all the time.

'Your visits are never a problem, Luca. I only wish I could persuade you to stay with me all night.' She sighed, meshing her fingers with his. 'It can't be relaxing for you, getting up to go back to your own suite every night. You don't need to do it. I know better than to make any claim on you. It would give you a complete night's rest, too.'

'Don't worry about me,' he assured her. 'In any case, I'm not due to go into the office until tomorrow.' Raising his hand, he carefully brushed a stray strand of blonde hair back from her brow.

'You have some time off? But according to your schedule—' Beth looked away and began scrabbling for her bag, but he caught her chin and turned her face to his again.

'I cancelled,' he whispered. His voice was like melted milk chocolate. 'I thought we could try a little extra rest and recreation in the bridal suite this afternoon.'

Leaning forward, he gave her a long, slow kiss. And it took Beth's breath away.

'But—but I thought this arrangement of ours was only lasting for as long as our trip…' she said faintly.

'It will last for as long as I want it to,' he murmured, kissing her again. Beth's hand went to his hair.

'Now we are back in Venice, you will sign a new, permanent contract with Francesco Fine Arts. That will give you financial security for as long as you want to go on working here. You're a good student and I can't take the risk of you flouncing out at a moment's notice. As a fully contracted staff member of Francesco Fine Arts, you'll be able to apply for formal courses to broaden your experience. Although I hope you won't object if I continue some of your education myself…'

His hand slid up to caress the smooth skin between her stocking and panties. Beth closed her eyes. In Paris, she had been overcome by a physical need for him so strong it had scattered all her guilt and fear in an ecstasy of desire. But now she wondered whether things were going too far. The rational part of her brain said she ought to put an end to everything now, before he found someone else and hurt her yet again…

'Are you all right, Beth? It isn't like you to be so quiet.'

She opened her eyes. He shot her a look of concern that was an echo of his voice. It surprised her.

'Yes—I'm fine, thanks. It's just that…I don't want you to be accused of favouritism, Luca. Now sex is back in the equation, I'm not sure how to react when I get back to the office.'

'Sex—so that's all it is for you, this time around?' Luca picked up on the word straight away. His expression hardened, challenging her to deny it.

Beth felt adrenalin flood through her veins in a tingle of danger. A warning note in his voice alerted every nerve in her body.

'I thought this was supposed to be a fresh start for us, Luca. We agreed to forget the past.'

'Yes, but the past has a way of forcing itself to the front of my mind now we're lovers again, *tesoro*.'

'You are your own man, Luca. You always have been. Why should I be looking to pin you down now, when we've been there, done that and suffered all the consequences?'

'And I have the scars to prove it,' Luca growled.

He pulled away from her. Settling back in the driving seat, he started the car. He did not need to watch Beth running her fingers through her hair or fiddling with her clothes to realise she was uneasy. She might be saying one thing, but Luca's very male instincts told him she was thinking quite the opposite.

'It's in your nature to seek commitment, Beth. You come from a fine English family. Your people are expected to suppress all their emotions in favour of making a good marriage.' He set out the truth as he saw it. 'You know from experience I won't be forced into a relationship, and you're not sure you can go through all that again.'

She leaned her head against the passenger window of the car. There was no point in trying to deny it.

'I can't change the past, Luca. All I can do is try and influence the future.'

'And you can only do that if I let you.'

It was the fear she had never dared to face. Now he was making her confront it.

'I know I can't expect anything from you, Luca. It would serve me right if you ended up treating me as badly as I treated you, that night back in Balacha.'

'Revenge is not what I am after,' he stated firmly. 'And this is *nothing* like a one-night stand.'

After a pause, she found the courage to come out with

something she had wanted to tell him for a long time. There might never be another chance to open her heart, so she had to do it now.

'I was never really unfaithful to you, Luca. There was nothing physical between Tristram and me. But I had to choose between loneliness with you, and a sympathetic ear from him. I could either spend my life forever waiting for you, or accept second best. Back then, a man who never travelled further than the office coffee machine looked like the better bet for a "normal" life.'

'You always deserved better, Beth,' Luca said brusquely, appearing to concentrate on the traffic rather than her.

Yes, but that was then and this is now, Beth thought, feeling an agony of tears build up behind her eyes.

'But you have set yourself free from all that now, free to fly with me for a while,' his voice interrupted her thoughts quietly. 'I always tried to get you to cast off convention. This arrangement of ours has proved you're willing to try, Beth. You are right—you have changed. The first time I saw you walk into the executive lounge of FFA, my heart went black and cold. I thought you were the same girl who preferred weddings to work. But seeing what you have become has taught me something about myself.'

He stopped, and she saw his knuckles whiten as he gripped the steering wheel. She braced herself for a shock. When it came, it was far more of a surprise than she could have imagined.

'I've discovered I have a weakness. It's for you, Beth. It always has been. I know that now.'

Beth was so amazed she could not speak. He shot a glance across the car's interior, laughing at her confusion.

'So why don't we forget all about commitment, and fly together for a while longer?'

They connected—and for a fraction of a second it was an almost spiritual moment. Their minds came together—but then he had to switch his attention back to the road. Beth had no distraction. Her mind could absorb his words while her body revelled in the thought of having first call on him, for at least a little while longer.

Her reaction spread to Luca. Out of the corner of his eye he saw she was moving in the seat beside him. Her hands opened and closed in a helpless gesture, as though she did not know what he wanted her to say. Tiny wordless sounds came from her beautiful, inviting mouth.

'You don't need to answer straight away, Beth, unless the answer is no,' he said in a voice low with feeling.

Just the nearness of him had an effect on her; it was all she could do to restrain herself. He was talking about sweeping her off to paradise. When Luca was involved, it could be nothing less. In suppressing a moan of desire, she rocked forward in her seat and her eyes closed momentarily. When she opened them again, her gaze connected with Luca's in a spark of recognition.

Wordlessly, he reached across the central console of the automatic car and took her hand. If he was honest with himself he had stopped being interested in casual sex the moment Beth had walked back into his life, but could he put the past behind them? Their clasped hands hung together for a moment as he fought the impulse to draw her fingers towards his body. With growing excitement, Beth saw he was as aroused as she was. The formality of the black linen business suit and stockings she always wore while travelling felt far too constricting. Perfectly attuned to the sound of her silken underwear brushing against the lining of her skirt, Luca's hormones almost got the better of him.

'Sit still!' he commanded with a glint in his eye. 'It's hard enough trying to keep my mind on the road as it is.'

This was the point of no return. Beth had to risk her heart, throwing it out to him in the hope he would catch it. Whether he kept it safe, or merely tormented it, hardly mattered any more.

'Then why don't you turn off the road right now, Luca?' she whispered.

'No…' He stretched the word out with relish. His attention might have switched back to the road, but his hand had fallen into her lap. He was gently caressing the curve of her thigh through her thin skirt. 'What I have in mind for you needs space and time. I am going to kiss you all over, *tesoro,* from the tips of your toes to the tips of your fingers, and everywhere in between.'

She moaned again. 'Luca, stop…I can't wait…'

He smiled, and pressed his foot to the accelerator. 'And neither can I. Let's get home.'

When they got to the palazzo, Luca took her straight upstairs to the bridal suite. There he made love to her with a relish that closed over her like the night. Afterwards, they lay together in the afterglow caressing each other gently. Beth wanted the moment to last for ever. She stretched out in the huge warm luxury of the double bed. 'Tonight's experience has been better than anything I've known in my whole life,' she whispered, relaxing into the warm security of his arms. 'For the first time it felt as though you weren't holding anything back, Luca. I thought I'd sacrificed the chance to be happy like this.'

He did not reply. With a smile, Beth realised he had drifted off to sleep. So she whispered, 'I never imagined I could experience actually being loved by you like that, but here I am.'

She woke in darkness, but still in a dream. For the first time, Luca had stayed beside her into the darkness. Until now, he had always left her shortly after sex. The most he ever did was doze for a few minutes, with her in his arms. Then he would leave her. Sleeping together all night would make things too permanent, he said. He *always* made a point of going back to his own bed.

Unable to bear the thought of him leaving her this time, Beth made herself stay awake. All she wanted to do was snuggle into him, but she resisted the temptation. The moment he tries to leave, I'll ask him to stay, she thought. But Luca slept on. Tonight, unlike other occasions when she had seen him with his eyes closed, he looked totally at peace. His breathing was slow and regular. When he moved, it was only to mould his body closer to hers.

Luca slept so deeply that eventually Beth's mind began to lead her astray. When she checked the small travel clock on her bedside table, she saw it was almost four o'clock in the morning. He *never* stayed this late in any bed. An early riser, he spent the hours before work in his gym, or the length pool. He would probably wake at any moment, ready to swing into his morning routine.

A frisson of excitement dared Beth to do something

reckless. What if she anticipated him? She could creep away and slip into his bed. When Luca woke, he would think she had gone into her own bathroom, and leave without disturbing her. But there would be a surprise waiting for him, back in his own room!

Smiling, she eased her way out from within the protection of his arms. Not taking her eyes off him, she reached for her robe and pulled it on before padding out into the silent corridor.

The door to his suite was not locked. Beth walked in, breathing deeply. Masculine fragrances of sandalwood and cypress filled his reception area. Alert to every sound, she stopped once or twice on the way through to his bedroom. Every creak, every rustle made her look back over her shoulder, but she was still alone. Without switching on the light, she crossed to the shadowy rectangle of his bed. Pulses pounding, she launched herself onto it with a gasp of delight, but a sudden rattle and crash almost made her heart stop.

She had knocked his bedside table, sending everything on it clattering to the floor.

She froze, expecting somebody to rush in and confront her. Nothing happened. The loudest sound in the room came from her thundering heart. After waiting for it to steady, she started groping for the bedside light.

Blinking in its glare, she saw a confusion of things lying on the floor where they had fallen. There was a small black box, a fold of paper, and what she took to be a large coin. Climbing off the bed, she knelt to see if she had done any damage.

It was not a coin. It was a medal. Reading the details

engraved on the reverse, Beth discovered it had been awarded to Luca for extreme bravery. Unfolding the sheet of paper, she discovered what he had done to deserve it. The first shock was the date mentioned in the citation. It was the same day she left Balacha for the last time. She read on with growing horror. Despite terrible injuries, Luca had gone into a burning building to save one of the rebel soldiers. It must have happened straight after he piled me onto the last plane to leave the airfield, she thought. A place he fought to keep open, so she could survive. Her last image of that terrible time was the sight of Luca, plunging back into the firestorm she was leaving behind.

Everything fell into place. Her blood ran cold. He must still be suffering from the injuries he received that night. It was why he was on medication. At their first meeting in the executive lounge, Beth had been shocked by his pale, drawn face. She had seen the agony in the expressions he tried so hard to hide.

'I never wanted you to see that.'

Beth jumped violently. It was Luca. He had entered the room quietly, and she hadn't heard him. The sound of his voice surprised her so much the presentation box almost hit the floor again. Terrified, she looked over her shoulder. He was silhouetted in the doorway, one hand resting lightly on its frame. When he did not shout or rush forward she realised he was disappointed, rather than angry.

'Why didn't you tell me about all this, Luca?' she said softly.

'I didn't want it to make a difference. You might have seen me differently.'

Beth didn't know whether to be relieved or worried by his calm acceptance.

'But it would have explained such a lot! About those tablets you take, for a start, and I imagined all sorts of awful things when you said you'd left the army. It never once occurred to me you might have been invalided out.'

'So, now you know.'

'Yes. Yes, I do—and do you know what? You were right. It *does* make a difference to the way I feel about you. A very big difference.'

She put the medal back in its box, and replaced it on his bedside table. Then she turned to him, and put all her deepest hopes and dreams on the line.

'There's a part of your life you want to keep to yourself. That must be why we've always made love in my bed, never yours. And it explains why you've never really let me touch you. All I've ever wanted is to feel your warm skin against mine. It explains why the lights are always low, or you've kept my hands off your body. Why you won't stay the night in my bed. I thought you wouldn't let anyone close because I had wrecked your mind. Now I realise what I did to you must have wrecked your body, as well.'

He shook his head. 'It wasn't all down to you, Beth. I had a choice about that.' He nodded towards the medal in its velvet-lined box.

'Is it very bad?' she said quietly.

'Bad enough.' He sighed, and walked over to the bed. Sitting down on it slowly, he leaned forward and rested his arms on his thighs. 'Although the headaches are easing off at last.'

'Is that what the tablets are? Painkillers?'

'Some of them—others are to compensate for spending my life stuck in an office,' he finished grimly.

'That must be why you haven't needed to take so many since we went to Paris. The pressure wasn't so bad, away from Venice.'

'Yes…I suppose so,' he said.

'So why do you carry on doing a job you hate?' Beth challenged him.

He looked at her intently. 'Because so many people depend on me.'

'I don't.'

Still on her knees, Beth worked her way over to where he sat, and reached up to put her arms around his neck. When he turned to her, she leaned her head against his.

'Once I've learned all I can from you, I shall be off, Luca. You won't need to fret I'm getting too attached to you. That's one worry off your list, at least. I shall soon be off to England to make my fortune in the antiques trade— ha, ha,' she added with irony.

'You're really determined to do it?'

Beth found she could not meet his eyes. Moving her head slightly, she buried her face in his hair. She was trying to swallow her desperate need to hear him say the words *don't go*.

'Yes.' She managed to sound firm, but she was dying inside. 'I've always promised I'll never need to rely on you again, after this. Although…if you ever feel like telling Francesco Fine Arts where to go, I'll invite you to England and you can be my gigolo, instead.'

He put his arm around her waist and pulled her close.

'You,' he said with slow amusement, 'have a very vivid imagination—'

Beth nodded, unable to speak

'And a flair for this work I never suspected,' he finished.

'I have to work, Luca. It stops me worrying about you—'

She stopped, appalled. It was the worst possible thing she could have said to a man who valued his independence above everything else. For a split second they stared at each other. Teetering on the boundary between past and present, Beth waited for him to brush off the comment, but it didn't happen. All she could do was correct herself as fast as she could.

'I mean—it stops me worrying about whether I'm going to be able to pay off my father's debts before you sack me for trespassing in your bedroom, Luca,' she said in a rush, and then tried to laugh.

'I'm glad you're not worried about me.' He eased away from her, and stood up. 'Because I'm fine.'

'As long as you are.'

She clambered off the bed, sensing it was time for her to go. 'My mind started working overtime when you said you'd left the army. I was beginning to wonder what horrible truths you were hiding from me, Luca.'

'Nothing that won't keep.' He glanced at the clock on his mantelpiece. 'Especially as it's nearly time to start getting ready for work.'

Neither of them moved. Eventually, Beth could resist it no longer. Reaching out her hand, she laid it on the reassuring bulge of his bicep.

'In that case…why don't you take a shower with me

now, Luca?' she said impetuously. 'We always used to enjoy it so much.'

The room was dim, but she could still appreciate the look in his eyes.

'So I'm supposed to start taking orders from you, am I?' he growled.

It had no effect on Beth. She laughed softly.

'Only this one—and, in any case, since when have you taken any notice of orders? You were told not to take me to Balacha airport that night, but you did. After that, you were told to retreat from the airstrip, but you didn't, giving our pilot time to get away. You were under orders to stop the rebels, but now I see from the citation that you went inside the burning communications tower to save one of them—'

Luca kissed her into silence.

'You know your trouble, Beth? You talk too much.' He breathed against the silken skin of her neck.

She chuckled again. 'I've embarrassed you, and you don't even know what I'm going to say next!'

'How can it be any worse than what you've dug up already?' He half smiled, but stopped when he saw the look in her eyes.

'Come on, Luca. You used to love getting me in the shower.'

She looked at him steadily. His reaction was like quicksilver. He let her go and turned away.

'No.'

'It's because of what happened that night, isn't it?' She nodded towards the velvet-lined box on his bedside table.

Beth walked around to face him. Unconsciously, Luca

spread one hand across the taut expanse of his tee shirt, drawing it backwards and forwards in an instinctive gesture.

'All the bits you've let me see so far have been perfect, Luca.'

She went closer. Lifting one hand, she began stroking his hair, and then his face. When he did not stop her, she slipped her other hand around to caress the small of his back.

'I'm in your room. No one else can ever have got this far, or you wouldn't have left your medal out on the table. Why not let me be the first one to go all the way with you, Luca?'

She looked up at his face. He had his eyes closed. Beth smiled, taking time to savour the majestic lines of his jaw and the dark sweep of his lashes before she spoke again.

'You don't need to hide anything any more, Luca. To me, you're the most irresistible man on earth. And you always will be.'

He did not move a muscle. With a sigh, Beth leaned against him. After a while, she felt him rest his head against hers. They stood in silence. Neither could relax. Beth was too conscious of his taut frame. She knew it was a tension held between her own hands, that only she could release. Sliding her fingers beneath the hem of his white shirt, she began caressing the skin beneath. She soon discovered why he was reluctant to strip right off. At one time his chest and the small of his back had been completely misted with soft dark hair. Now she could feel bare skin slashing it in several places.

'Does that hurt?' she whispered to him as she touched the damage lightly, and felt him shake his head.

Taking his hand, she started cautiously towards his bed. To her delight, he followed. They lay down together in the darkness. Rolling his tee shirt up a little bit at a time, she kissed each centimetre she revealed. When she reached his armpits, she stopped.

'I've always told you this thing gets in the way. Why don't you get rid of it now, Luca?'

He did not react immediately. For minutes on end they lay together in silence. The rise and fall of his chest was the only movement he made for a long time. Then he sat up, pulled the tee shirt off over his head and threw it aside. Beth sat up, too. Curling her body around his, she used her lips to test all the parts of him that he had kept hidden from her until now.

'You don't mind, Beth?'

'When have I ever minded kissing you?'

He made a strange noise, and she looked up sharply.

'Sorry, did that tickle?'

'I'm not laughing.'

'Do you want me to stop?'

'There isn't much sensation in the scar tissue,' he began as she continued her gentle exploration of the pale streaks. 'Although…that still feels good…' He sighed into the silence.

'Shall I start running the shower, or will you?' She smiled between kisses.

The last taboo had been broached. There were no secrets between them any more. Time whirled past for Beth as Luca taught and guided her during the day, and then took her to heaven every night. His pride in what she was achieving at work was only matched by her respect for his bravery.

Then one day Silvia the housekeeper arrived for work in a worse mood than usual, and Beth plummeted back to earth with a crash.

'*Natale* is less than a month away, so I suppose signor will be cluttering up the house with a flock of guests as usual. Me—I'm expected to guess, these days! He hasn't told me a single thing. Has he said anything to you?' The housekeeper pierced Beth with a glare.

'*Natale?*' Beth recoiled from a bowl of yoghurt on the buffet and chose a pear and a glass of water for her breakfast instead. It meant Luca would be teasing her again about her ravenous appetite over dinner, but somehow she could never face eating much for breakfast any more.

'You know, the birthday of the baby Jesus?' Silvia flapped her hands as she translated her way through more complaints. 'Not that the seasons mean anything to anyone any more. *Beccas* put up their window display in October—I'm surprised you never noticed!'

Beth hardly heard, because there was something else she hadn't noticed—and it was serious. While Silvia grumbled on, Beth sifted through her handbag. Her diary was right at the bottom. Grabbing it, she flicked through its pages first backwards and then forwards. Recently, her stomach had been a bit delicate in the mornings. As she began counting days, and then weeks, it shut down altogether.

There might be a very good reason for the vague symptoms haunting her. Unusual feelings had been ebbing and flowing through her for a while, but Beth had been managing to ignore them. Now she began putting two and two together—and it made for a disaster.

She had been drinking nothing but mineral water for weeks. Both wine and coffee tasted odd to her now. She was always tired, and veered from starving to queasy. She had been putting it all down to excitement, and not enough sleep. But now her diary was hinting something else. Because she hadn't seen a period since leaving England.

CHAPTER ELEVEN

AS SOON as she could sneak away to a distant pharmacy, Beth bought a pregnancy-test kit. The result was a formality, and everything fell into place. It explained her exhaustion and the strange feelings she had been experiencing. The thought of carrying Luca's child made her heart bounce—but only as high as the ceiling of reality. She would have a permanent reminder of Luca to cherish, but her excitement was almost crushed by the thought of having to tell him.

This was totally unplanned and unexpected. Beth had no idea how it could have happened, but she knew exactly how he would react. Time after time, he'd made it crystal-clear he would never be cornered into a relationship. It had taken so long for him to relax in her company again… News like this would destroy all his trust in her, once and for all. She had worked so hard to convince him she wasn't just another scheming woman, after his fortune. Now nature was doing her best to prove otherwise.

Of all the things that could have happened, this was the one guaranteed to turn Luca against her for ever. Beth had tried to trap him into marriage once before. He would *never* believe this was a genuine accident.

She sat alone in the reception room of her suite. Staring at the test result without seeing it, she wondered how she could possibly break the news to him. It would wreck the perfect little world they had created together over the past weeks. There were no secrets between them now—except this one, Beth thought hopelessly. Luca had shown her all the damage done to him, that last night in Balacha. With everything out in the open, she had been able to ease his mind that her plans for the future didn't include hitching a free ride. She had shown him, too, that his physical scars made no difference to her.

Beth had always thought it would be impossible for her to love anyone else the way she loved Luca. But as she sat there in her suite a subtle change started to creep over her. She loved him just as much as ever, yet powerful emotions built up as she thought of the new life growing inside her. Her baby was part of Luca. He would hate it, but it was something she would protect and nurture for as long as she lived. She closed her eyes, trying to make sense of everything. When she opened them again, the first thing she saw was the beautiful rug Luca had bought her in Paris. It was laid out in front of the reception room hearth, replacing a far more expensive antique. It's totally out of place here, like me, Beth thought.

She looked around the rooms that had been hers for such a short time. *When Luca hears about this, memories will be all I have,* she told herself, trying to relive every moment. She wanted them printed on her mind for ever. This room was where she had made that first, tentative move on him, the day he had first shown her around. He had been rigid with scorn then.

Only a few minutes ago she had left him stretched flat out in his own bed, fast asleep. He looked totally relaxed today, like a lion at rest. Beth had been able to kiss him and ruffle his hair, with no response.

She stifled a sob. It would be her last moment of intimacy with him. He wouldn't want her now.

The more she tried to hold back her tears, the more pain rose up in her chest. It threatened to burst out in a wail of anguish. Every second she spent in this rose-scented hell made the agony worse. She had to get away.

Cramming a few things into a case, she ran downstairs and slipped out into the damp, dark, early morning. Leaving the palazzo meant losing Luca for ever, but she owed it to his child to be strong, and do it. All her life she had expected other people to take care of her. Now it was up to Beth to take responsibility for something—her baby. Luca wouldn't want to support her, and she didn't intend cramping his style. They had both been free spirits, once upon a time, but that was over for her.

Beth had to hope two things would eventually soften the pain of losing Luca. One was the thought he would be able to go on living this life he had chosen, without needing to worry about her. The other idea that kept Beth running was that she would be protecting his unborn baby. Until now, she had always managed to pass the responsibility for her actions onto someone else. That time had passed. She knew it was far better to hide her heartache for ever than to see it reflected every day in Luca's face.

* * *

Venice was already filling with wintry smells: weeds, water and sodden wood. Beth's trip to the airport passed in a dismal, rain-spattered blur. Even the sky is crying, she thought, dragging herself into the shelter of the airport building. It took her a long time to make any sense of the departure information. Her mind was too full. All she could see was Luca's expression, if he ever found out about their child. She wanted to save him that, but it was killing her.

She went over and over his warnings in her mind. He never wanted to be tied down. He had enough commitments already. He had no time for marriage. Beth had known all that from their earliest days together. When their first relationship had collapsed, she had accused Luca to his face of not being the marrying kind. He had agreed. This time around, she had signed up to his idea of an arrangement based on sex without strings. And yet somehow, knowing what she knew and doing what she had done, she had *still* let this happen!

Memories gouged pieces from Beth's heart. As she paced around the departure lounge dangerous thoughts began to form in her mind. She had been mad to walk away from him the first time. Perhaps pregnancy had altered her state of mind again? Luca was a proud man. Perhaps she should have forced herself to tell him the truth from the first moment they had met at FFA. If she had explained straight away she had always loved him, and wanted to stay with him for ever, it might have changed things. The worst that could have happened was that Luca threw her out straight away. Instead, she had tried to hide it and they had grown closer once more, like new skin meshing across an open wound.

This baby was sure to burst them apart again, with no hope of any repair. Ever.

Beth's heart began to pound, dragging her breath in great silent sobs. If only she could open her heart to Luca now, bloody and battered as it was—he might take pity on her. Was it too much to ask? She couldn't bear to think of the endless longing. His unborn baby was the only thing she had left in the world. What chance would the poor child have if she turned her back on its father? Only a little while ago, the thought of exposing her deepest feelings to Luca like this would have been unthinkable. Now it was far too late. Beth knew she should have done whatever it took to keep him. But now she could never go back. She would never see him again—

'Beth?'

Nobody spoke her name as beautifully as Luca did. It was the last place she expected to hear his voice, but it was unmistakable. She stopped, and whirled round.

There he was. His midnight-dark hair glistened with raindrops, and he was breathing fast as though he had been running.

'Luca?' His name whispered from her lips, then jumped out in a shout that turned every head for metres around. 'Luca! What are you doing here?'

'You forgot something.'

They stared at each other.

Say: Me! You forgot me! Beth willed, but he didn't. Instead, he trapped her with the magnetism of his gaze. He watched her wordlessly for a long time, as he had done so often before. He looked to be on the brink of making some great speech, but no words came out. Eventually, he put his hand in his pocket and pulled something out. Handing it to Beth, he waited for her to supply the words.

'It's the necklace you made for me!' she said in amazement. 'But—where did you find it? I thought that was long gone. I tore it off and threw it away.'

'In Balacha, yes,' Luca said. 'I picked it up.'

Beth stared at him in wonder. 'And you've kept it safe for me, for all these years? But…why wait until now to hand it back?'

His expression hardened as she tucked the souvenir away in her bag. He looked around, and caught the attention of a uniformed man standing nearby.

'Please could you arrange for someone to retrieve Miss Woodbury's luggage?' he called.

The man grimaced. 'That's not my job. Luggage is nothing to do with me. You'll have to—'

'I am Luca Francesco, Managing Director of FFA.' Luca silenced him with deadly intent. 'You will have Miss Woodbury's things loaded into my Mercedes immediately, or I'll want to know why.'

The man blanched and scuttled away. Luca took hold of Beth's arm, and escorted her towards the exit.

'I don't like pulling rank, but this is a special case. The alternative is to pay bribes, which I despise.' His face was impassive. 'You are coming back home with me, Beth. Now.'

His words tore strips from her heart. 'Oh, Luca…I—I can't…'

'Why not?'

'I—I need some time alone. You've always been so keen on keeping your independence. My time in Venice has made me realise how important that is to you. I've started to feel I need it too. Emotional space is something neither of us will have while we're both living under the same roof.'

It was all lies. She had to gulp down air to stop the truth screaming out.

He stopped. He looked her up and down. Then he let go of her arm and began prowling around her. His relentless dark eyes scrutinised her. Beth felt a shimmer of fear. Could he sense it wasn't only the hormones of desire fuelling her now? Did she look different already?

'I've noticed you've been quiet for a while,' he conceded. 'But this running away is such a drastic move— and so sudden. Why didn't you mention these feelings last night?'

'They come and go.' Her voice sank, like her spirits.

'But they were particularly bad, first thing this morning? Bad enough for you to drop everything, abandon me and leave a letter on our breakfast table?' His brows knitted together in a thunderous frown.

He must be about to guess. I can't let him know! Beth thought in a mad panic. Summoning up all the courage she had, and some she'd never known she possessed, she rose to his challenge.

'No...' Beth began hesitantly, but managing to say that single word gave her enough nerve to look up at him directly again. 'No—actually, it was last night when I decided we were getting too close.'

A lump rose in her throat. She choked back her pain and battled on. 'I kept it to myself, put a brave face on things and thought it all over. Then I got a good night's sleep.

Things usually look better by daylight, but today, for me, they didn't. I decided a clean break would be best for both of us. My idea was to cut out all the awful argument and agonising that went on in Balacha. But now you've followed me here, and spoiled everything. I didn't want this, and neither should you. So let me go, Luca!' she finished defiantly.

He stopped pacing around her, and stood silent for a moment. If Beth hadn't known better, she would have thought he was cranking up the tension to see how much more she could take. Was he determined to see her collapse in a tearful confession? It was starting to feel like that. Beth balled her hands into fists. Digging her nails into her palms, she willed herself to be strong. She had to—for the sake of the little life growing between them.

While Luca scrutinised her Beth's eyes darted about, looking for the quickest escape route when he decided to release her from his gaze.

'No. That explanation doesn't convince me at all, Beth. Why do I get the feeling you aren't being entirely honest with me?'

His expression was fierce. His lips were a narrow, angry line. She shrank beneath his stare. They stood in the middle of the concourse, two individuals trapped in time. Luca's watchful silence went on and on. And on. Beth felt a trickle of perspiration run down between her breasts. She knew how single-minded Luca could be. He would stand there for as long as he thought she was hiding something from him.

She had to get away. Even if it meant losing one of the mementos of him she had been determined to keep.

'All right. You've beaten me again, Luca. I confess.' She opened her bag and took out a small, heavy object carefully wrapped in tissue paper. 'You've given me back my necklace, so you ought to have this in return.' Handing it over to him, she stood back, out of his reach, as he peeled back the tape.

'My Rolex.' Hefting the watch in his hand as though estimating its value, he shot a look at her.

He shook his head, puzzled. 'How did you get it back?'

Beth rolled her lip. 'It was never lost. Watching the street kids at work in Balacha taught me a lot. While you were distracted at that crowded newsstand in Paris, it was the easiest thing in the world to take it off your wrist.' She hung her head in shame.

'You stole it? But why?'

'Luca, you were killing yourself! You were working too hard, and too stressed out to look after yourself properly—I had to stop you being such a slave to time. And it worked, didn't it?'

He smoothed down the front of his new suit, and considered what she'd said. His tailor had been the first to notice the change in him, but now it was obvious to everyone. Luca had put on some of the weight he had lost, he was spending less on prescriptions, and his last health check had been nothing but a formality. He couldn't remember the last time his back had seized up, or he had been flattened by a migraine. That left more time for exercise, which in turn made him feel better about indulging occasionally. It was something he had only just started doing again. So, yes, he had Beth to thank for all that.

'I'm sorry I stole your watch, Luca,' she muttered. 'It's been preying on my mind ever since I did it.'

'But you didn't think to leave it behind with your note, when you left the palazzo?'

She shook her head. 'I wanted to hang onto it. As a keepsake of you—as if I needed a reminder.'

His expression changed. Instead of accusation, his gaze became searching. It threatened to strip out the last of her secrets, exposing her very soul.

'And is that your last guilty confession?'

She nodded, eyes downcast. Despite everything, she could not feel any guilt about their baby. The poor little thing hadn't asked to be conceived.

'There's nothing else you want to tell me? Nothing that might make me stop you getting on your plane?' Luca persisted.

'No—no, Luca…you must let me go…' She tried to turn away, but he caught her firmly by the arms and pulled her back.

'Not this time.'

His face was alive with conviction.

Beth looked down, conscious of an unusual feeling. His fingers were working into the skin of her arms, but that wasn't the reason for it. Luca saw her grimace. Thinking he was the cause, he released her instantly.

'You are not leaving my country unless you can look me straight in the eyes and tell me that you want to go. That you want to leave me.'

His words wrung another confession from her, but it was not one either of them expected to hear. 'Oh, Luca, I'm leaving because I *do* love you, and I always have! I've never stopped loving you, not for a second. That's the truth—but I know it's the last thing you want to hear, so now you'll *have* to let me go. Please…'

His hands moved to her shoulders and for long, agonising moments he held her at arm's length, searching her face. It was as though he was making up his mind about something. Then in a characteristic flash of impetuosity he pulled her into his arms and kissed all the breath out of her.

Hungry for all the kisses she would miss, Beth responded. People milled past, but the two of them were alone in each other's arms. Nothing else mattered. The sheer power of their love pulsed through them again like a wave, but it was interrupted by a pang of pain. It clutched Beth where she should have been feeling only pleasure, and made her break away from him with a gasp.

Luca was not about to let her go. 'Beth…I've come to take you home,' he whispered into her hair, his voice husky with passion. 'And this time, no arguments.'

The spasm passed. 'Yes, Luca,' she managed, because she could say nothing else.

'It doesn't sound as though you'll put up much of a fight.'

'No, Luca.'

Beth knew there was no way she could get onto a plane now, feeling the way she did. I'll try again tomorrow, she told herself. I'll be better then.

She was unable to think straight. Only the feel of Luca's hand beneath her elbow gave her enough strength to stay upright.

He led her all the way through the building, but Beth was in such turmoil she was hardly aware of the journey.

She would not have been able to deny him if she had wanted to. He looked magnificent. His jaw was set, and he strode through the airport as though absolute mastery was as natural to him as breathing. As they reached the main doors Beth began shivering uncontrollably. Luca's flinty expression instantly softened with concern.

'You're cold.'

'I'm dressed for a flight, not a kidnapping!' She tried to laugh, but had to quickly press a hand to her side.

He shook his head. 'I'm not doing anything I shouldn't have done the instant you walked back into my life, Beth.'

Her heart was so full she pulled his hand up to her lips and kissed it. In reply he put an arm around her shoulders and drew her closer. They walked over to where his Mercedes was waiting. When Luca spoke now, he was holding her so tightly she felt his words resonate through her body.

'Marco! Miss Woodbury is feeling the cold. Turn the heater right up—oh, and find your own way home, would you?'

He pulled a bundle of notes from his pocket and peeled off a sheaf, which he handed to the chauffeur. Marco responded with a broad smile, saluting smartly as he opened the passenger door for Beth.

Unable to bear a second's separation from her, Luca slid into the driver's seat before she had finished fastening her seat belt. His next words were whispered between simple, reverent kisses.

'I've wasted far too much time, Beth. I sent you away from Balacha because your happiness meant more to me than my own pain. When you left me again this morning I knew I had to get you back, no matter what…' His voice died. He turned away from her and began concentrating on backing his car out of its parking space. When his attention went back to Beth, it was his turn to gasp. She had fallen forward, her arms wrapped protectively around her waist. A faint sheen of perspiration glittered on her brow.

'Beth? What is it?'

When she could answer, she spoke without looking at him. 'I have a pain.'

'Where?'

She couldn't reply. Something was squeezing all the life out of her. The only thing she could do was draw her hand back and forth, low down over her groin.

'*Mio Dio!*' Luca hit the accelerator like a man possessed.

CHAPTER TWELVE

BETH sat in the car, shaking with cold and fear and anguish. Luca parked his Mercedes crazily in a forbidden zone outside the hospital. Rushing round to the passenger side, he bent to take Beth in his arms.

'Thank goodness,' she panted. 'I don't think my legs can carry me.'

'Put your arms around my neck, *tesoro*.'

He reached into the car and gently lifted her out. He winced in pain momentarily but was quick to mask it so Beth didn't notice. Within seconds he was rushing her down a corridor that smelled of disinfectant and disaster.

'Luca, no…you've taken a wrong turning. The sign said it's this way to maternity and gynaecology. I must be an emergency—'

'Exactly.'

He rapped out the word. Before Beth could react, a woman doctor rushed out of a side room and greeted Luca by name. She was still pulling on her white coat, but made time to smile at Beth. The orderly with her brought a wheelchair for Beth.

'Miss Woodbury?'

'That's right, but how do you know who I am?'

'Signor Francesco rang me at home. *Buon giorno*—I am Donata Bruni, his personal physician.'

Beth thought she had reached rock-bottom, but one glance at Luca's beautiful, smiling woman doctor brought new meaning to the word 'despair' for her.

'So why are we in a women's department, if you're Luca's doctor?'

'It's the best place for you.' Luca answered for Donata.

His tone was so strange that, despite her pain, Beth made herself look up at him. 'But what about all the doctors and nurses who work here already?'

'They will have to get used to working with Donata while you are here,' he said sharply. 'Everyone does what I tell them, when it is as important as this.'

'People must get appendicitis every day,' Beth said through gritted teeth. She was saturated with perspiration, and clenching her fists so hard her fingers ached almost as much as her stomach.

An explosive curse from Luca startled both women into silence. Spinning the wheelchair round, he seized Beth by the shoulders.

'How much longer can you keep up this act?'

'As long as it takes,' she whispered.

The doctor cleared her throat pointedly. 'I think you'd better go back to Reception for a moment, Signor Francesco. There are admission forms that need to be filled in. I'm sure Miss Woodbury would like all that paperwork taken off her hands.'

Luca looked from doctor to patient, then back again. It was the first time Beth had seen him look so pale and sick since her arrival in Venice. She felt her lower lip starting to tremble.

'Could you do it for me, please, Luca?' she said in a small voice.

He nodded.

'Yes. Yes, of course.'

His head dipped forward as though to kiss her cheek, but at the last moment he stopped. Releasing his hold on her shoulders, he straightened up.

'I'll be back as soon as I can.'

There was no point in trying to answer him. He was already several metres away, striding back towards the reception area.

'Can I take it you don't want this baby, Miss Woodbury, as you've been denying it so furiously?' the doctor said quietly as she wheeled Beth into a side room. Beth was horrified.

'I want it more than almost anything I've *ever* wanted!' She gasped. 'But Luca mustn't know I'm pregnant!'

'It's a bit late for that, I'm afraid.' Donata sighed as she scrubbed up, ready to examine Beth. 'He told me you were losing his baby.'

'B-but…why on earth would he think such a thing? How can he know I'm pregnant?'

Beth closed her eyes. No torture in the world could be worse than this. Luca knew, and she hadn't been the one to break the news to him. He had known she was lying to him, all through that scene in the airport. Now it was too late to explain why. She turned her face to the wall. She had lost him. He would never trust her again after this.

* * *

Luca did not come straight back. Beth had to explain and cry in the treatment room alone. Much later, an orderly arrived and began taking the brakes off her bed. She assumed he was going to evict her from the hospital, out onto the street. Instead, he pushed her into a private room full of flowers. She was speechless. Luca arrived as the orderly was leaving.

'Why didn't you tell me about the baby straight away?' His deep voice carried across the room from where he stood in the doorway.

Beth looked down, unable to meet his gaze as she answered, 'Because I knew you wouldn't want it.'

'So you tried to get rid of him?'

'No! Never!' Forcing herself up from her pillows, she wailed in agony. 'If you'd let us escape back to England, you need never have known—'

Almost as if against his own will Luca crossed the room towards her. 'I was his father. I had a right to know,' he said softly. He had been absolutely convinced from the first moment that any baby of his was bound to be a boy. In his mind, there could be no doubt about it. He could have had a son.

Ours should be a team of three.

In those few precious minutes between their reunion in the airport and the start of their tragedy, Luca had been trying to mould a new future in his mind. He was certain his son would have been the tallest, darkest, most handsome hero of the Francesco line. He was destined to be clever too, and a real asset to his father—exactly like Beth. While he had been waiting for her to confess, certain that she would, Luca had begun to think that her pregnancy might have been the best thing that could have happened between them. His own parents had lived hard and died young, chasing pleasure. As a result, he had sworn never to become too attached to anyone. Yet the instant he had seen Beth again, he had changed his mind. In a split second, he had realised the way to lasting happiness lay in commitment, not escape. He needed Beth—for ever. They were a team. That was how life should be.

And then, within seconds, his strange new future had collapsed. Now he had nothing left—except the knowledge that the woman he wanted ran away from him because she was scared he didn't want their baby.

'You may have had a right to know, but you had absolutely no right to make our lives a misery!' Beth sent a blaze of raw emotion streaking across the room to meet him. 'And that's exactly what would have happened if I'd told you, Luca! "No commitments," you always said.'

Luca walked slowly to her side. 'You didn't tell me, Beth. At the airport I did everything but come straight out and ask you, but you *still* didn't tell me…'

'Because you didn't really want to know.'

Beth's voice was an arrow of ice, and it hit its mark. He turned away from her and silence hung in the air.

Then, in a voice she thought barely strong enough to reach him, Beth found the courage to speak. 'Luca…now you know everything. But tell me, how did you find out?'

He looked back at her. 'After I discovered your letter at breakfast, I went straight up to your suite to see if you had packed everything. Or if there was a chance you might be back.' He paused, raking a hand through his hair, then went on. 'There was a scrap of packaging on the floor beneath your table. It was small, but big enough to tell me I woke up alone this morning because you were doing a pregnancy test.'

Beth rolled over and buried her face in her pillow. It was already drenched in the fragrance of exotic flowers, which covered every shelf in her room. For ever afterwards that rich scent would remind her of what happened next.

'I would have loved him,' Luca said with quiet authority.

Beth turned her head. She spoke to the ceiling, rather than risk letting him see the truth hurt her all over again.

'Really? I didn't think you could possibly love anyone.'

When he didn't reply she looked across at him, but he didn't meet her gaze. There was something about his lack of response that made her think.

'You kept my necklace,' she said slowly. Freed from the pain and panic she had suffered at the airport, all sorts of details were coming back to her now. 'You've sent me all these flowers…and you're still wearing the watch I gave you, so long ago. *And* you stopped me leaving for England…'

Her voice was becoming stronger by the second. Luca stepped in to prevent her from going any further.

'Of course I did. I could hardly stand by and watch while you walked away from me a second time, could I? Especially as you were carrying my son.'

'Oh, Luca…'

She burst into tears again, but this time he was there to catch her. This time he held her tenderly, telling her that one day—not today, not tomorrow, but one day—everything would be all right again. 'You are the only one who matters now, *tesoro*,' he murmured into her hair.

But as her tears stopped, and she started to feel safe in his arms, Beth felt him pull away from her. He stood up from the bed and began to pace the room. When she looked up at him she saw his face contorted with despair.

'Luca…?' she whispered.

'Why did it have to happen to you? To me?'

'Luca…come back. Hold me.'

He responded to her plea so fast, Beth was being scooped up in his arms before she knew it. His body was taut and hot beneath the silk of his pristine white shirt. She rested her cheek against it and let her fingertips slide down and around his waist, holding him close. She could feel the life force throbbing through him. It raced at a terrific rate, reminding her of how much she inspired him.

Gradually the adrenalin ebbed away. When his pulse steadied, she spoke into the silence.

'Luca…'

There was no response.

'Luca?' She tried again. 'It doesn't have to be like this. You don't need to be a slave to the past. You've proved it once already, by rejecting everything that happened between us in Balacha. This could be the start of something wonderful…if you want it to be…' she whispered, hardly daring to put her hopes into words.

He shook his head, torn apart by conflicting emotions. 'I've never stopped wanting you, Beth, though God knows I've hated myself for it sometimes. But it's more than that now. What happened here today has shown me how fragile life is and how I've got to make the most of every second. Marry me, *mio tesoro!*'

She blinked. 'What did you say?'

Beth could hardly believe it.

'Marry me. From today, FFA will have to do without me. I'm taking a non-executive role until you're better. We'll have an extended break at Rose Cottage. And if it's what you want, we'll live there permanently while you design us that brand-new house you've always wanted.'

'But…what about the tradition? You can't leave the palazzo, Luca—there's been a Francesco in residence for more than five hundred years.'

'Some things are more important, especially to an Italian man,' he said with growing passion. 'I need you, *carissima*. Nothing else matters to me now.' His eyes burned into her.

Beth steeled herself. She had to bring up the one thing that had single-handedly torn them apart and brought them back together again. There was no getting away from it.

'But…what about our baby?' she whispered, blinking quickly to hold back her tears.

Luca's strong, bronzed hand closed over hers as she twisted the crisp white hospital sheet.

'I'll speak to Donata. Perhaps in a little while…we can try again?' he said, with a rare hint of diffidence.

Beth frowned. She looked into his face, puzzled.

'You mean—you haven't spoken to her already?'

'No. I walked around for a while, and then I went to the florist's. It took me some time to make it back here, and I didn't want any more delay. I wanted to see you straight away,' he said.

She could only guess at what it had taken him to return.

'So…you still don't know that all this was a false alarm?'

Luca went as white as Beth felt. His lips moved, but for once he was lost for words. She put a hand to his hair, calming the unruly waves. Impetuously, she took one of his hands and pressed it against her waist. She got her reward. His fingers spread across the smooth plane of her belly as pride and wonder filled his expression.

'Then we are to have a second chance?'

She nodded, unable to speak for happy tears.

'After all I've put you through—' He shook his head. 'Can you find it in your heart to—Beth, we can start all over again? From the beginning?'

She looked into his eyes, and didn't need to answer. Her expression said it all. His slender olive fingers danced restlessly over the stiff white sheet covering her, hinting at uncertainties he would never put into words. With a smile, she touched his hand.

'Of course.' As she looked into his eyes all her doubts disappeared. 'I've dreamed of nothing else, Luca.'

Slowly, and with all the tenderness she could have wanted, he kissed her. Afterwards, his breath escaped in a long sigh.

'I will make up for everything, Beth, and for all the time we've spent apart. From now on, I'm going to treat you exactly as you deserve. I'm going to shower you with roses, lavish you with everything you could ever need and kiss you over and over and over again—'

She silenced him with a kiss of her own, sweet and gentle.

'Then I really will be your little *principessa,*' she whispered, 'although all I've ever wanted is your heart, Luca, to treasure for ever.'

He lifted her hand to his lips and kissed it.

'It's yours,' he said tenderly.

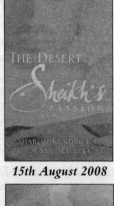

Celebrate 100 years of pure reading pleasure with Mills & Boon®

To mark our centenary, each month we're publishing a special 100th Birthday Edition. These celebratory editions are packed with extra features and include a FREE bonus story.

Plus, you have the chance to enter a fabulous monthly prize draw. See 100th Birthday Edition books for details.

Now that's worth celebrating!

July 2008

**The Man Who Had Everything
by Christine Rimmer**
Includes FREE bonus story *Marrying Molly*

August 2008

Their Miracle Baby by Caroline Anderson
Includes FREE bonus story *Making Memories*

September 2008

Crazy About Her Spanish Boss by Rebecca Winters
Includes FREE bonus story
Rafael's Convenient Proposal

Look for Mills & Boon® 100th Birthday Editions at your favourite bookseller or visit www.millsandboon.co.uk

4 FREE

BOOKS AND A SURPRISE GIFT!

We would like to take this opportunity to thank you for reading this Mills & Boon® book by offering you the chance to take FOUR more specially selected titles from the Modern™ series absolutely FREE! We're also making this offer to introduce you to the benefits of the Mills & Boon® Reader Service™—

- ★ **FREE home delivery**
- ★ **FREE gifts and competitions**
- ★ **FREE monthly Newsletter**
- ★ **Exclusive Reader Service offers**
- ★ **Books available before they're in the shops**

Accepting these FREE books and gift places you under no obligation to buy, you may cancel at any time, even after receiving your free shipment. Simply complete your details below and return the entire page to the address below. You don't even need a stamp!

YES! Please send me 4 free Modern books and a surprise gift. I understand that unless you hear from me, I will receive 6 superb new titles every month for just £2.99 each, postage and packing free. I am under no obligation to purchase any books and may cancel my subscription at any time. The free books and gift will be mine to keep in any case.

P8ZED

Ms/Mrs/Miss/Mr ....Initials ....
BLOCK CAPITALS PLEASE

Surname ....

Address ....

....

....Postcode..

Send this whole page to:
UK: FREEPOST CN81, Croydon, CR9 3WZ